She Held the
by His Should

He had no strength to fight her. He was weakened by the loss of blood. Pinned by her hands and the tone of her voice.

"You will lie still, please, and do as you are told."

He stared up at her. "You don't understand. They will be coming for me."

"Who?" Gwynneth asked.

"The men with the guns."

"You don't need to worry about them. They don't know you're here and we're not going to tell them."

His eyes closed again. He couldn't go. Whatever he said, whatever he'd done, he couldn't go. He wasn't meant to be shot or captured. He was too beautiful. . . .

"What have you done?" Gwynneth asked. "Spying is it?"

"It was a routine observation flight," he said.

"What's your name?"

He opened his eyes to look at her. "My name is Erlich," he said. "I come from Eridani Epsilon."

"Where?"

"Eridani Epsilon. Eleven light-years away across space."

STAR LORD
Louise Lawrence

PUBLISHED BY POCKET BOOKS NEW YORK

POCKET BOOKS, a Simon & Schuster division of
GULF & WESTERN CORPORATION
1230 Avenue of the Americas, New York, N.Y. 10020

Published by arrangement with Harper & Row, Publishers
Library of Congress Catalog Card Number: 77-25674

ISBN: 0-671-82959-9

First Pocket Books printing January, 1980

10 9 8 7 6 5 4 3 2 1

Trademarks registered in the United States and other countries.

Printed in the U.S.A.

To Ann
Because there are no words

It was mild at the end of March and the valley was thawed, gray-green and dismal under low cloud. Rhys stood by the window. A track led upward from the farmyard and he wanted to go. The mountains were hooked in his nerves, tugging him. He wanted to walk the long humped shape of the Brechin. He wanted to tread the mood of the Mawrrhyn. Blod sat with her head on her paws, patient, watching him. Her tail wagged expectantly. She knew Rhys would go.

The old man coughed by the kitchen stove, and smoothed the pages of a newspaper.

"I'm going out, Grandad."

"You go, boyo."

"Be all right, will you? On your own?"

"Managed all right on my own till you came."

"They'll be back in less than an hour."

"You get on. Never mind me."

"I'll take Blod then," said Rhys.

Hywel Thomas nodded.

"Aye, you take her, the two-faced bitch!"

"Just for a spot of fresh air," said Rhys.

But Hywel Thomas knew more than Rhy understood. He knew when the Mawrrhyn called. He had lived all his life in the reach of those hills. He was old now, and the damp got to his chest, but the compulsion was in him, the same calling, strong inside. He knew why Rhys wanted to go. She was more than just a mountain, rock scarred by glaciers, heaved up from the stone-dead land. She was alive. The soul of her lived, wild and untamed and ruthless. The Mawrrhyn was a place without pity.

"You mind her."

"Who? Bold?"

"The Mawrrhyn."

"Been there enough times by now, Grandad."

"Mind how you go, that's all."

"I'll mind," said Rhys. "Don't think I'll go to the Mawrrhyn anyway. I'll go for a walk along the Brechin instead." He zipped his anorak. "Come on, Blod."

He found the sheep in a shallow gully.

He was alone on the mountains and he had to try.

"I'm sorry, girlie."

The yellow eyes stared at him, dumb and glassy.

"Once more," said Rhys. "Just once more."

He gripped, pulled gently, tried not to hurt.

The lamb came suddenly, dragged free with a rush of suction, lay inert on the grass, steaming in blood and slime. Stillborn, thought Rhys. But it had not been dead inside the sheep. He had felt it move. Do something, Rhys thought. The sheep bleated softly, nuzzled her lamb and started to clean it. It twitched feebly and convulsively.

"Do something!"

The mountains were all around him, empty and covered with cloud.

Only Blod sat waiting.

"What do I do, Blod?"

Her tail thumped once. She couldn't help him. Hywel Thomas had trained her well. Blod wouldn't go near a yeaning ewe. But she knew Rhys was in trouble. Her eyes cared, brimmed with the sorrow she felt for him, deep brown and utterly useless.

"Useless!" said Rhys. "You're flaming useless! What do I do?" He stared around him. He could feel the Mawrrhyn brooding. "What would Grandad do? Think, you fool!"

Breathe into it, life into it.

— Rhys pushed the sheep aside, cradled the lamb, small like a child, still warm, still living, still just living. He could see what was wrong with it. It was born with a caul across its nose. He pulled away the thin, sticky membrane, wiped its face roughly on his jacket, then blew. He felt it jerk, once, twice, start to struggle. It would go on living now. He gave it back to its mother.

"There you are, missus. One cuckoo lamb. Next year have it in the right place at the right time and don't rely on me for your luck."

He wiped his hands on the grass, moved away to sit on his haunches and watch. He felt pleased with himself. More than pleased. He wanted to dance, run wild, laugh with relief. It was over, the terrifying first time. Over, the controlled fear and the sweat. He had birthed a lamb all on his own. It wasn't born breached, dead on the mountains. It was alive. He had broken the harsh laws of the Mawrrhyn. And the silence touched him, sharp as a claw, thick and cold with the mating of sky and stone. Powerful. Rhys was alone in his defiance. But not quite alone. He heard the hum of an airplane high and far away.

"One day," Rhys said, "you're going to be damned."

He talked to the mountain but he should have been talking to Blod. He was seeing a lamb and he should be seeing her. She thrust her face between his knees, licked the traces of blood from his fingers. Her brown eyes gazed up at him, pleading, adoring, asking to be noticed. There was a humming in the sky which hurt her ears. She whined softly, telling him. But he wasn't thinking of her.

"You wait till I tell Grandad."

Blod whined, pushed against him.

"My first lamb."

Whined.

"If we hadn't stopped by it would have been dead."

Whined. Pushed. The whole of Blod loving into him.

"Don't!"

He swayed and overbalanced. Wet grass soaked him, sphagnum moss soaking his trousers. Blod licked, cold nose, warm tongue dripping, licking his face, his eyes.

"Get off, you stupid dog!" Licked. "Get off!"

He pushed her, angry.

"Get off!"

There was sheep shit all down his sleeve.

"Now look what you've done!"

Blod slunk away, tail between her legs, belly to the ground. She crept in a wide half circle up to the track and stayed there, looking down at him. He might have beaten her. She looked beaten. Her eyes were terrible with all the hurt and rejection she felt, all the deep brown love he hadn't wanted. She was leaving him.

And the great brooding presence of the Mawrrhyn came rolling down on him, all the loneliness of the high places and the silence unbroken by the far cries of sheep, the tumble of water, and the high-pitched humming of the plane. It wasn't a plane. It was as if the sky itself were humming. Rhys looked up at the gray cloud and the thin veils of rain. He could see nothing. The Mawrrhyn trapped him in the sound and the silence. He was condemned by Blod's misery, left with the crime he had done to her, alone in a vast, primordial jail. And the humming was everywhere over the sky and the land.

He felt the first stir of terror.

"Blod! Don't go!"

She slunk a few paces, hesitated, looked back.

He was a mess anyway. It wasn't her fault.

"I'm sorry, Blod. But don't go, don't leave me."

She came to him then, to the tone of his words and his outstretched hand. Crawled, tail wagging slowly. She was wet in his arms, smelling strong, forgiving him. And he loved her in the sound coming closer, in the gray vibrating air. Blod the dog. Two-faced bitch, the old man called her. She was his, really. But now, by the laws of affection, she belonged to Rhys. Belonged in the sound pitch, in the shrill, endless humming that seemed to drill through his brain until it was everywhere, inside and outside of him, and Blod whined with the pain. He covered her ears.

"What is it?"

It tore down the sky, ripped fast and unbearable.

"What is it!"

Noise. He couldn't stand it. Blod howled and Rhys knew what would happen. He held her through the few last fragments of seconds. Then the thing struck. He felt the impact come through the mountain and into him. And the boom of the sky went on and on down the valleys until it faded away. There was a landslide, rock and boulders falling. Scree sliding softly. A trickle of smaller stones. And finally nothing, just the endless tumbling of water and the sheep shifting down in the gully, a scutter of her hooves on the ground.

Rhys got to his feet.

Nothing changed on these changeless mountains.

But something terrible had happened on the other side of the Mawrrhyn.

2

The bus dropped them by the roadside. Llanysted, the village was called. There were thirteen houses, and a post office-shop in Mrs. Owen-Morgan's front room. There was a postbox set into the garden wall, saying G.R., and the window advertised DeWitt's Backache Pills and Brooke Bond Tea, but the *o*'s were missing. They had been missing since 1949, when Hywel Thomas' daughter left for Cardiff. Now she was back again. Enid Williams her name was now.

"Did we get stamps?"

"I did," said Gwyneth.

They had a mile or more to walk to the farm along a lane with a sign that said: TO THE MOUNTAIN CENTER. Gates in dry stone walls led to flat fields of bitten pasture where beef cows breathed mist into raw air. Spiders' webs draped last year's grasses, and rooks were building nests in the elm trees down by the chapel. Out where the lane curved wide around the foot of the Brechin, a terrace of cottages crouched at the dark edge of a forestry plantation. Half-grown firs rose in ranks, gave way to the moors and the mountains that were invisible up ahead. It was a dreary landscape. Gray and lonely. The wheels of the shopping cart made fine jets of spray. Their footsteps sounded loud, and traffic on the main road dissolved behind them.

Gwyneth put down the heavy basket to change hands. The desolation seemed to cling to her.

Enid knew. "Not much for you out here, is there?"

"I don't usually notice," Gwyneth said.

"Not much for any of us out here."

"I expect it's the weather."

"We should never have come."

"Oh, Mom! Don't say that!"

Enid sighed. "Sometimes I can't help but feel it."

Gwyneth looked at her. She had aged these last months. Her face was lined and her hair was going gray. She'd taken it hard. She didn't say much, but it showed in her eyes. Like now: She wasn't seeing what was out there, she was seeing inside herself. And what she saw was all bitter, remembering and blaming, regretting what they'd done.

But Gwyneth wasn't sorry. She wasn't sorry they had left that other house and the man who was her father. Even though she liked Cardiff, liked the streets and the shops and the lights, and hadn't wanted to leave, she couldn't be sorry. It was better here. The hate was gone. There was no anger. No quarreling, no silences, no hurtful remarks. It was lovely, really. Lovely when the curtains were drawn of an evening and they all sat around the fire. Mom knitted, Grandad talked with Rhys, and Blod whined in her dreams. They had each other in a way they had never had before. Lovely.

Awful, too.

Gwyneth knew how awful it could be. A horrible place. The stove had fits of smoking. You had to light the boiler in the scullery for hot water and bathe in a tin tub. The walls flaked and the kitchen stank of dog, and Rhys tracked mud over the flagstones. You had to go through the garden to the lavatory, and that stank too. Things got on all their nerves—running out of flour, with the store so far away . . . having the handle break on the pump . . . men all over the house, bringing in the electricity . . . and the old man turning crochety . . . and the mountains outside . . . and the weather. There was no escaping. No way you could get away from the perpetual rain and the mountains.

"We'll get used to it, Mom."

"It's all so primitive."

"It'll be better when we get the bathroom."

"If your grandfather ever agrees."

"He let us have the television."

"He hates changes."

"He doesn't hate us," Gwyneth reminded her.

Enid smiled slightly. "No, he does not hate us."

"Well then, we're better off, aren't we?"

She was so certain.

"Don't you ever feel you're missing out on things?"

Gwyneth put down the basket. "Look, Mom, why don't you stop worrying? We're all right, me and Rhys. And it's not as if we have to stay here for all time. I'll be taking my exams in June. I can start nursing at Cardiff General just like I planned. Nothing's really changed."

"Hasn't it?" Enid looked thoughtful. "What about Rhys? Your brother has changed. He always said he was going to college to be a teacher. Now he says nothing, just talks sheep with Grandad. What will he do then? Or hasn't he said?"

Gwyneth frowned. "He hasn't said."

"But you know," Enid prompted.

"I think he might take over the farm."

"Yes," said Enid. "That's what I was afraid of."

"I don't see what's wrong with it," said Gwyneth.

"Don't you? Do you want to see Rhys end up like the old man? Do you want to stand and watch him waste his life? It's the dead end he will be making for himself."

Gwyneth stared ahead at the vague gray mountains. Damp clung to the tendrils of her hair. She heard the hum of an airplane far away. Was it wasting a life out here? Would it be a waste if Rhys chose it?

The old man told stories of winter nights, how there were legends about those hills. How, if you listened, you could hear the voice of the Mawrrhyn in the wind. Magic, he said. Gwyneth heard and felt nothing of that magic, but Rhys did. It was like a passion with him. He felt free out there. He had found the ice ages scratched on the rocks. He had lost himself in vast geological eons. Rhys loved those mountains.

Hywel Thomas loved them too, and his life wasn't wasted. He kept up his trousers with a piece of string, slept with his shirt on, cared nothing for culture and modern conveniences and what went on in the world. But he cared for other things. He cared when the tourists went traipsing over his mountains, when the sheep got sick and Dafydd Jones' nephew was missing on the moors. He had a strange way of knowing, did Hywel Thomas. Not much book learning, but something deep, like an instinct in him. He read the signs. Signs of the earth and the sky, signs in people's faces. That day last November when the three of them had knocked on his door, he hadn't had to ask questions. He had just looked at them and known. It wasn't a waste, that kind of knowing.

"It's not wasting," Gwyneth said.

"Then what else is it? Out all day roaming with an old man and a bitch . . ."

"Blod, Mom. And he's loving it. That's not waste."

"It is, the way I see it."

"Not so much waste as your loving," Gwyneth said.

Enid didn't answer. Her lips went tight and she watched the sky. There was a humming sound over the Mawrrhyn. And Gwyneth was sorry she had spoken. Sorry for the hurt. It was enough to reach anyone, this gray, wet, godforsaken place. The only modern things in sight were the pylons strewn over the fields. The only modern sound was in the sky.

"I'm sorry, Mom."

Enid stared upward. She looked afraid.

"Mom? What's wrong?"

"That noise."

"It's only a plane."

"It is not."

"Damp on the wires, then."

"There are no wires out there on the Mawrrhyn."

But it had to be something, some kind of machine. A huge dome of sound was filling the sky, collecting over the mountains. They could feel the air vibrating, the ripped scream in the clouds as the thing tore through them and down. They stood together, clung. Enid's fingers gripped tight on Gwyneth's arm, wanting comfort. Her voice choked.

"Oh, God, it's too low. It won't clear the ridges."

"Don't say that, Mom."

"It's going to crash."

"No, Mom! Not here! Not to us!"

Enid broke away . . . ran with giant strides, pulling the cart.

"Mom!" Gwyneth screamed. "You can't do anything!"

The crash killed her voice as the thing struck. The

feeling of impact came rolling down the valley and over her in a great boom of sound that the sky spread, to be heard over miles out beyond Brynllan. Gwyneth felt it in the ground; the shock wave fled up through her shoes and into her. It was actually in her, the ending out there on the mountains with the rocks falling, and the scree, until the echoes in her head let it go and a cow coughed somewhere in the silence.

Ahead of her, Enid still ran.

"We can't do anything, Mom!"

"We can try."

"They'll be dead!"

"We can't be certain."

But Gwyneth was certain.

No one could have survived that crash.

3

It had been blasted, a whole area of mountain, like a great black scar on the flank of the Mawrrhyn. Rhys stood at the edge of it. Grass and heather still smoked. Heat devils danced at the center of the fire that had burned and died into bare earth. His boots disturbed puffs of hot ash. He couldn't walk into that black center of heat. Nothing could. There was nothing alive in the pit of the crater. Clouds drifted over it like a shroud. The falling dampness touched and turned to steam. There was a sadness in Rhys. He had never seen such total devastation.

Somewhere behind him a stone shifted.

Blod was whining but he did not move.

Something troubled him.

There was no wreckage. The slope within his sight was empty. He could see nothing of any plane or machine. No twisted undercarriage, no bodywork, no broken tail section. Something had crashed here, something huge and fast, powered by an engine, driven down. But there was no wreckage, no clue to what it had been, no charred skeletal shape looming, no person within the mist. But Rhys knew things didn't disintegrate completely, vanish without trace. There had to be something.

He started to search, working in a wide circle around the crater. It wasn't hard to find. Fragments of pale metal were everywhere, tiny broken shards among the grass and rocks and heather, always within the radius of the center. It was as if whatever it was had exploded on impact, split outward from the core of itself like a shattered light bulb, and there was nothing left of it but splinters. Rhys held them in his hand, dull silver splinters of something he didn't recognize. He stared down the gray dimension of the other valley. Whatever it was had come from that direction. Whoever it was.

"Who are you?"

Suddenly and very strong he felt the grayness hid the living answer, that someone had escaped and was needing to be found. But there was no sound anywhere under him and Rhys could not hold the feeling. It seeped away. His reason told him that no human being could have survived that crash, and the cold, ruthless presence of the Mawrrhyn let no one live. Her silence itself was termination, and only Blod broke it with her small, incessant whines.

Rhys pocketed the pieces of metal and went to her.

"What is it, girlie? What can you see?"

She could see nothing. She gazed into a vague gray distance with lost eyes. But she sensed more than he did, she trusted her sensing. It was out there somewhere, Blod knew, something hurt, something she mourned for.

"Where then? Where is it, Blod?"

She didn't look at him. She was telling him.

It was out there where her crying was.

"Down there, is it? Someone?"

Rhys went, but he didn't believe her. He couldn't. Or maybe he could and did. Animals had strange ways of knowing. It wasn't for nothing that Blod was leading him. He felt slightly sick. Sick at the thought of what he might find. Smashed metal was inanimate. He could cope with that. But smashed flesh . . .

"Why me?" Rhys asked.

They must have heard it. Everyone must have heard it, in Cwmvanwy, Caeravon, and Brynllan. They were bound to come, the police, and the forestry, and the ambulance. They would come up the peat track over the moors behind the Brechin, and he wouldn't have to wait long.

Blod made for the lake at the head of the valley. Rhys saw the waters stretching dark and wide and deep. Dead reeds bent over their own reflections, rain pockmarked the surface. Then the clouds swept down from the mountain and everything was gone. Rhys moved by memory and Blod was crying to him, her dog voice mourning among the reed beds, dragging him deeper in. His feet sank in the ground, disturbed the stench of the bog.

"Anyone here?"

Nothing answered, only Blod calling him. And when he reached her, her eyes had a vacant, puzzled look, as if she had forgotten why she'd come. If it was scent she'd been following, the waters had taken it, or it had been lost in the vile, reeking quagmire that shifted around her. Rhys knew he could spend days searching this place. A nesting coot fled with a rattle of wings. The reeds closed him in. Then Blod found it . . . the dead body of a sheep.

She sat there looking pleased and satisfied. Rhys

floundered. He wanted to be angry with her but he could only be glad. Glad. He was thanking God, in that stinking bog, that it was only a sheep that had died. Even the putrid process of decay seemed sweet, like a miracle.

"You great steaming idiot, Blod!"

She looked at him quite calmly, looked at the sheep as if she expected it to move.

"That's not what we were looking for!"

Ooze crept over the tops of his Wellingtons. Rain soaked his hair.

"Come on, nut case. Let's get out of here."

He led her back to the higher slopes, where the rain slashed his face, made rivulets between the stones, and the sound of the stream was swollen and filling all the valley. The cold and the wet was through to his back, and Blod's fur was filthy and sodden. Whoever came wouldn't search far in this weather.

"You bitch!" Rhys said to the Mawrrhyn.

He stood again on the charred edge of the circle. The black heat was dying and the crater stayed empty. There was nothing anywhere but the small fragments of metal. If there had ever been a person, he must be assumed dead. There was nothing Rhys could do but go home.

But Blod did not want to go. On the high crest of the Mawrrhyn, she was whining and looking back. The feeling had returned to her. Someone was out there, by the lake, wanting her to go. She whined, telling Rhys, trying to explain.

"No," said Rhys.

Whined. Pleaded.

"No! Come on!"

She followed him reluctantly. She wasn't happy and he knew it. She was being torn. Part of her was wanting to go with him, and part of her was wanting to go back. But he wasn't searching through bogs for her, wasn't going miles for the look in her eyes and her crying. Nor was he taking a census of dead sheep. Blod sat and whined.

"There's nothing down there," said Rhys.

Whined.

"If you used your common sense you'd know there was nothing. If anyone was in that plane, they've got to be dead."

Whined, she did, sad and miserable.

Rhys squatted, held her face.

On either side of him the valley fell away.

"Don't cry Blodsy. We've done all we can. It couldn't have been manned, because he wouldn't have had time to bale out, and have you ever smelled burned flesh?"

Perhaps she believed him. Perhaps something in his voice got through to her, that he did care but he wasn't going. Or perhaps she heard the sound of men and Land-Rovers coming over the Brechin and trusted them to find what she had failed. She went with Rhys, of her own accord, down into her own valley. But the mourning was still there, the faint, sad crying in her throat. And Rhys heard them calling, their voices in the cloud, calling . . . his mother, and Gwyneth, and the old man.

There was nothing they could do, any of them.

He pulled out the fragments of metal he had kept. Studied them. Eggshell-thin, fragile pieces, absorbing the warmth of his hand. Whoever heard of a plane made like that? And the men were coming, the rescuers, coming to the wreck on the Mawrrhyn. Rhys shook his head.

"So what was it, then? Experimental?"

4

Enid piled chopped vegetables into a saucepan for making soup. She was wearing boots and an apron was tied over her raincoat. The kitchen was hot from the fire and the doors were open to let out the steam.

"I'm going down to the village," Gwyneth said.

"What for?" Enid asked.

"Stamps," said Gwyneth.

"We got stamps in Brynllan."

"Except that I forgot them," Gwyneth said.

They could not stay inside, any of them, not with the happenings going on. They had to be outside and part of it. Rhys sawed firewood in the yard, and Gwyneth went to Mrs. Owen-Morgan's because it was happening down in Llanysted too and she wanted to be there to hear about it. Only Enid was missing things, cut off by the walls of the room.

She went through the hallway to stand on the porch.

It wasn't afternoon or time that she was aware of, but the voices of men on the mountains and the excitement in the air, tight like a strung wire all the way to Brynllan. A police car went along the lane with a soft swish of wheels. She heard it turn off onto the track through the forestry plantation. Another one joining the search. Behind her, the soup boiled over. She pulled it to one side, tilted the lid, and left it to simmer. She could not stay inside.

Rhys was in the outhouse, stacking wood.

"There's another police car gone by," Enid told him.

"I don't know what they hope to find," said Rhys.

"They must be hoping to find something."

"Red tape in triplicate probably."

Enid measured two scoops of grain into a bucket.

"Suppose there was someone in it?"

"There couldn't have been."

"But suppose there was?"

"Then he's dead," said Rhys. "Shall I feed the fowls?"

"No," said Enid. "I'll do it myself."

"It's raining."

"Never mind. I would rather be out than in. Fill the boiler for me, will you? We'll have baths this evening."

There was a walled paddock behind the house, almost a part of the mountains, yet Enid could see nothing. But the stillness was electric with feelings, and all over the valley the people would be out. She could feel them, like herself, their eyes and minds clamped on the mountains where the searching was, waiting and wondering. But the cloud banks hid the Mawrrhyn, hid the knowledge. There was only a thin calling of voices that were high and far away.

Enid rattled the bucket.

The fowls rushed around her, pecked at the scattered corn. Fowls did not lay well in damp weather but she had to check the nest boxes in the dark sheds. And once again the walls cut her off. She stooped in the smell of droppings. Dust rose from dry straw and cobwebs clung to her hair. She did not know what she was missing, what might be happening in the few minutes she was gone. The door jammed on her way out. Forcing it left green stains down the side of her raincoat.

She came around the corner, carrying the eggs in the bucket.

There was an army truck parked outside the gate, and a man in uniform crossing the yard.

He was going to the house, but he stopped when he saw Enid and came toward her. He was tall and smart with a military mustache, and she was not dressed to meet him. Inside the scullery Rhys stopped pumping water but he did not come to her rescue. He was listening in the gray silence and she was alone with the man.

"Captain Willoughby-Smythe, madam. Ministry of Defense."

"Good afternoon. Can I help you?"

"Is this an official road through your yard?"

"It is a public right-of-way, yes."

"So it's all right if I bring the truck through?"

"If you are going to the scene," said Enid. "It is best the other way. A better road."

"According to our survey map this way is quicker."

"It is more direct perhaps."

"Cuts off a good couple of miles, I'd say."

"Yes, but . . ."

"Then with your permission . . ."

Enid shrugged. "Oh, certainly. Come through this way if you wish."

The man smiled, left her, propped open the gate with a stone for the truck to come through. She went to close it behind him. But the back of the truck was full of soldiers who whistled at her and she did not know why. She was not Gwyneth. But all the same the whistling pleased her, like something lost was returning to her, and she was busy about the yard, watching until the truck had gone away into the cloud. She smiled as she heard the labor of its engine droning upward. He had been nice, that army captain. She was still standing there smiling when Rhys came out.

"There's excitement, Mom."

"Yes, isn't there."

"Did he say what they thought it was?"

"I didn't ask him."

"Must be military, though, or they wouldn't be here."

"I suppose it must."

"Ministry of Defense, he said. I bet it was one of their guided missiles gone wrong. You might have asked. For someone with your experience, you were slow off the mark."

What?" said Enid.

She was staring after them and her face was lined and worried. The clouds had fallen. There was a white, thick wall of mist rolling down the track, curling around the barns, creeping toward them.

"He should not have gone," Enid said grimly.

"Who? Willoughby-what's-it?"

"He should not be walking the Mawrrhyn in that murk."

"You don't know him, Mom. He might be a seasoned climber."

"They don't need his help up there."

"Who are you talking about?" Rhys asked.

"Your grandfather," Enid said.

"He's known these mountains all his life."

"Yes," said Enid. "But the Mawrrhyn has no pity."

5

Hywel Thomas knew the mountains better than any man.

"You won't find anything, Grandad," Rhys had said.

But he had gone just the same. Taken Blod and joined with Dafydd Jones and the other men. But there was nothing to find and the mountains were growing dangerous. You could not search blind in a mist that would not let you see. Only fools roamed the crags of the Mawrrhyn when the clouds were on her, and they did not need the help of an old man and a dog to fall and break their legs.

He came home in the late afternoon when Enid had changed into a blue skirt and sweater and was worrying about the mist and his cough getting worse. He came with Dafydd Jones in the forestry truck down the long track by the Brechin. He was met at the gate

by Rhys, who thought he might be Gwyneth, and
Blod was in a funny mood. She gave them both a re-
sentful look and slunk off up the yard.

"What's up with her?" Rhys asked.

"Whatever you done to her, boyo."

"I didn't do anything."

"Well, that's how she has been . . . skulking all
afternoon."

"Queer."

Rhys stared after her.

The old man pulled off his boots on the porch.

"You're back then," Enid said from inside.

"Aye."

"Found anything, have they?"

"Nope. And they won't, not in this weather."

"I was about to send Rhys to look for you."

"What do I need persons running after me for?"

"You're not as young as you used to be."

"I ain't decrepit either. Where's that danged dog?"

"I'll fetch her," said Rhys.

He went looking for Blod. But he could not find
her among the barns and outbuildings of the farm,
and she did not come to his whistling or his calling of
her name. She had gone to sit at the rise of the track,
with her face to the mountains, but Rhys was not
looking for her there. He returned to the house without her.

"She won't come."

"She must please herself, then," Hywel Thomas said.

The old man sat in a chair by the stove. The door to
the fire was open and he held his hands to the glowing
flames. Steam rose from his socks and his clothes were
dark with damp. His face had that ruddy look of one
who is always out of doors but it was lined deep with
his age, and the cough was racking him as his lungs

breathed the heated air after the raw cold outside. He was tired when the spasm ended. He wanted to do nothing, simply sit where he was in the soup smell and the sound of the kettle singing. Sit in the long, slow warming of his bones. But Enid had other ideas.

"Come on, Father. Let's have those wet things off."

"Aye. In a minute."

"Now, if you please."

The old man sighed. "Weren't like this before you came."

"No," said Enid. "I can imagine. You would have dried with your clothes on you in front of a dead fire. Eaten bread and cold bacon and caught pneumonia."

"Ain't caught pneumonia in seventy-five years."

"There's always the first time. Here you are . . . trousers, vests, pants, socks, and shirt . . . everything warmed."

"Where's our Gwyneth?" Hywel Thomas asked.

"Out," said Enid.

"Always a first time to be caught naked," said Rhys.

"Shut the door, you," Enid said sharply. "We are not having it left open half the night waiting for that bitch to make up her mind. It is the proper place for dogs . . . outside. And there is plenty of time for you to change," she told the old man. "Our Gwyneth will not be back for a bit."

It was strange, as if with the closing of the door the day was suddenly ended, as if they had come in out of it and the room became sealed. Whatever happened outside on the mountains no longer had anything to do with them. The small parts they had played in it were over. Maybe it would begin again tomorrow, or maybe it was gone for good. To Rhys it all seemed as far away as history, a past occurrence he would remotely recall at some future time. Only one question remained

unanswered . . . he did not know what had struck . . .
but even that did not seem important. Time was significant again. It was five-thirty and he was hungry.

Enid cut bread.

"We don't have to wait for Gwyneth, do we?" Rhys
asked.

"It would be good manners."

"But she could be ages!"

"I will be having mine where I am," said Hywel
Thomas.

"You will come to the table with the rest of us,"
said Enid.

"Never bothered with no tables before you came."

"You're not slopping soup down that clean shirt!"

"Oh, come on, Mom," said Rhys. "It won't hurt,
just once."

"It is slovenly."

"Well, who's going to see?"

"If anyone should come by . . ."

"You mean Willoughby-what's-it on his way back
down?"

Enid shot Rhys a look.

"I shouldn't worry about him," Rhys said. "He
won't notice Grandad slumming it, with you in that
skirt. Did you know you had a run up the back of
your tights?"

Enid gave in gracefully. The old man had bread
and soup in his lap and his tea stewed on the stove.
Gray mist hung outside the window and it did not
seem real. The things they told each other were things
that had happened to other people in some other world.
It was not Rhys who had stood with Blod on the black
edge of the burning. Not Enid in her shabby raincoat
and boots who had talked with Captain Willoughby-
Smythe. It was not Hywel Thomas who had been with
the police and soldiers, scouring the slopes of the

Mawrrhyn with their radios and headphones and gadgets ticking.

"Ticking?" said Rhys.

"Ticking," said Hywel Thomas. "Tick, tick, tick, tick."

"You mean Geiger counters?"

"Soldiers with ticking sticks."

"You saying it's radioactive?"

"Tick, tick, tick."

"Yes," said Enid. "That's radioactive."

"And what good does it do them?" Hywel Thomas asked.

"It measures the level of contamination," said Enid.

"Silly," said Hywel Thomas. "Silly I call it. All them play-things. What good does it do? Tick, tick, tick. So they know the Mawrrhyn has the radioaction, but that doesn't help. They can't change her with their playthings."

Rhys sat perfectly still. He could hear the ticking, now in the room, the clock on the mantelshelf that ticked the seconds away. Radiation sickness. He felt the nausea start in the pit of his stomach, and his hands burned. Skin burns where he'd touched. He stared at them. They did not look marked. The lines of his life and his fate were not scarred. But the small pieces of metal in his anorak pocket seemed to shriek the symptoms of Hiroshima. The fear was in him. The memory of the mountain and the black ash, the beginning of his death. He tried to make his voice stay calm.

"I touched it."

"Touched what?" Enid asked.

"Them bits."

"What bits?"

"Bits. Up there . . . bits of it scattered. I touched them."

"What are you trying to say?"

"I'm contaminated! It's radioactive!"

"I should hardly think so," Enid said lightly.

"Ticking, Grandad said. That's why Willoughby-what's-it went tearing up there. It's a blasted nuclear warhead!"

"If it was," said Enid, "we would not be sitting here now. We would be dead of the blast or evacuated to a decontamination unit. You're not getting sick. You've just eaten too much. And your grandfather has been up there along with a few dozen others . . . there is nothing wrong with him."

"So what is it then?" Rhys demanded. "What is that thing?"

"I will tell you, boyo," Hywel Thomas said. "I will tell you what it is. It is English, that's what!"

English!

It was like a final judgment. As if being English explained the destruction and the violation. Hywel Thomas did not hold with the English, English soldiers with English accents and English boots tramping over his mountains as if they had a right to be there. He was living in the Dark Ages. Wales for the Welsh. But progress didn't come from worked-out coal mines, male-voice choirs and hymn singing in the gray Sunday chapels. Didn't come from leeks and legends, daffodils and scraggy tats. Just because something crashed, smacked at the guts of the Mawrrhyn, it had to be English, as if the sky itself were rotten out beyond Offa's Dyke. Rhys was about to argue when the door flew open and Gwyneth came rushing in.

"Guess what!" She capered around the table, hugging herself. "You'll never guess!"

"Did you get the stamps?" Enid asked.

"No, I forgot. Go on . . . guess."

"Why don't you just tell us?" Rhys said.

"We're on television!" Gwyneth said.

"Who?"

"Us. Llanysted, Mrs. Owen-Morgan and Cledwyn Hughes. On the main news. Now in a minute. I ran all the way to tell you in time. Let's go and watch."

"Well," said Enid. "Now there's a thing."

6

There had been glass, said Mrs. Owen-Morgan, when the windows broke in the blast, and slates from the roof smashed. She thought a bomb had dropped and the child had awakened screaming. A pile of cans had fallen from the shelf, and Wynn Griffith's cat had had a heart attack and died. Cledwyn Hughes had been out with the tractor when he heard it come down. A plane, he said, but he hadn't seen it because of the cloud, and the steers had broken into the spring wheat.

For two and a half minutes Llanysted was the center of attention after the strike in Coventry. There was a shot of a police car and the chief inspector saying that search conditions would be difficult. There was a view of mountains under cloud, and people out in the street, watching. Then it switched to the London television studio and was quickly dismissed.

"There is no report," the newscaster said, "of any

missing aircraft, either civil or military. What crashed on the Welsh hills this afternoon remains a mystery. The army is holding an investigation.

"In American today . . ."

"So much for that," said Rhys.

"We are none the wiser," said Enid.

"Either they don't know or they're not saying."

"It was good, though," said Gwyneth.

"What was good?"

"Seeing it all."

"A bit like in the war," Enid murmured. "In the bombing. There was not much of it here in Llanysted, but the people were out of the houses, talking and watching and being together when Cardiff burned."

"Aye," said Hywel Thomas. "You were eight then."

"There was a feeling," said Enid.

"There was a feeling this afternoon," said Gwyneth.

"Fear," said the old man.

"No, it wasn't!"

"Fear making a bond between people. Fear of the sound. They didn't know what was up there, what came from the hiding clouds. When there is no knowing about something, the fear is always there."

"I reckon it's Russian," said Rhys.

"Why?" asked Gwyneth.

"If there's nothing of ours missing, then it must belong to some other country. If it was Common Market, they would have said. But the Russians wouldn't. They wouldn't admit sending a spy plane over our mountains."

"Glyn said it was a flying saucer," said Gwyneth.

"Ah," said Enid. "So that's it!"

"What?"

"Glyn Morris. I thought it was a long time you were forgetting to buy a few stamps."

It was evening soon. They called off the search before it was dark because the mist was down on the mountains and they couldn't see. The farmhouse crouched in a thick gray gloom. The light from the kitchen reached out as a yellow beam blurred by dampness. Inside, the old man dozed with a newspaper over his face, but Rhys and Gwyneth and Enid listened to the sounds of abandonment . . . the police cars going back down the lane to Brynllan . . . the soldiers going home. The army truck halted in the yard. There was a quick exchange of voices and Enid, in her blue clothes, opened the door to Captain Willoughby-Smythe.

"Who did she say it was?" Gwyneth whispered.

"One of the army chaps," said Rhys.

"She acts as if she knows him."

"She met him earlier on."

"When?"

"Shut up," said Rhys. "I want to listen."

But Captain Willoughby-Smythe said nothing interesting. He only thanked Enid for permission to drive through the yard and said they would be returning the next morning but they would not trouble her . . . they would use the other track over the moors. In the meantime, he had left a few of his men camped at the head of the valley, in case she should hear sounds in the night and wonder. And was that her black-and-white sheep dog sitting all alone up on the rise?

Enid came in from the porch. Her eyes were black and vivid in the sudden brightness.

"Who was *he*, Mom?" Gwyneth asked.

Enid did not answer immediately. She looked at Rhys. "There's that bitch of yours . . ."

"I heard," said Rhys.

He went to fetch her, Blod the dog, out into the

growing darkness and the shifting mist. He went by instinct up over the ruts of the track. He could see nothing and hear nothing, but Captain Willoughby-Smythe had said there were soldiers camped. Why? What were they guarding? A thousand million broken fragments of Russian espionage? Or the mountain herself?

Rhys didn't see the point. The mountain did her own guarding. You could not go against the cold white breath of the Mawrrhyn, the power of stone and precipice and tumbling water. She had beaten them all . . . police, and army and searchers. Men had no power in this place. Rhys could feel the might of her, her ancient darkness brooding through the fog. His nerves tightened as a boulder loomed in his way. He was off the path.

For a few seconds he felt himself panic. The Mawrrhyn had no pity. She was everywhere, closing in around him. Mountain, water, stone, and sky. She would take him as she had taken that machine . . . she carried no survivors.

"Blod!" Rhys shouted.

High up the valley someone answered him, and nearer, Blod whined. Rhys made for the sound. She did not greet him. She sat with her back to him on the edge of the track. She was gazing upward and whining softly. She was telling him it was still there, what they had failed to find that afternoon. She was crying for the hurt and the waiting and begging him to go.

"You've got to be mad, Blod," Rhys told her.

She was not mad. She knew. Whined to him, asking his help for something unknown up there among the cold and lonely places. She wanted him to go into the dark dropping over him, among the crags and slopes where he could fall and break his neck.

"Yes, and my name's not Spiderman. So come on."

There were boots on the stones coming down the track.

A voice called to him:

"Who's there?"

"Now look what you've done!" Rhys said to Blod.

A flashlight hit him. A rifle was leveled at his stomach. Rhys faced the soldiers.

"I came for the dog," said Rhys.

There were two of them, asking him questions, telling him he shouldn't be there, they had orders to keep people away. He was angry because they had no authority. Hywel Thomas owned the grazing right. And he was angry because Blod turned cowardly, crawled behind the shelter of his legs. But when the soldiers left she would not come with him, she started back up the track.

"I've had enough of you, Blod!" He caught her collar. "You're going home whether you like it or not."

He flung her yards down the track. And Blod knew by his tone that he meant what he said. He could not do what she asked of him, so instead he must make her obey him. She went with her head down and her tail curled under her belly. There was no joy anywhere in her. There was no joy in Rhys either. He'd hurt Blod's feelings. And when they were home, she would not come into the room where the living was. She would not eat the food. She moped in the scullery and now and then she would whimper.

"Be quiet, you mucker!" the old man roared.

She did not cry again.

It was quiet in the shut house. A coal slipped on the fire and Enid's knitting needles clicked monotonously. A wood louse crawled from the baseboard and Gwyneth flicked the pages of a magazine. In the scullery the water heated with soft, strong sounds, and by the woodpile was Blod, her eyes watching Rhys through the crack in the door, her outcast silence tearing him apart.

"I forgot to mention . . . I birthed a lamb this afternoon."

"Ram or ewe?" asked Hywel Thomas.

"I don't know," said Rhys. "I forgot to look."

7

On Tuesdays, Wednesdays, and Fridays Enid worked as a receptionist for a firm of opticians in Brynllan, but the next day was Good Friday, the beginning of the four-day Easter bank holiday, so she did not go. No one went anywhere. The whole area was fog-bound. White mist pressed against the windows, coiled thickly about the house. The old man coughed, the stove smoked, Rhys was restless and Blod acted stupid, skulking off up the track each time she was let out. There could be no organized searching and they saw nothing of the army except a Land-Rover which drove through the yard to collect the camped men. But Dafydd Jones, who called on Hywel Thomas about the foot rot, said they had set up a mobile headquarters on the moors by the Brechin. But that was all they heard. In the mist nothing was happening, and Gwyneth had a headache.

On Saturday it was the same . . . fog outside, smoke in the kitchen, Blod shut in the scullery, condensation on the windows. A sightless, soundless, motionless gray void clung close to the walls, stifled and oppressed them. They were cut off from the world in a raft of a house where they could not escape each other. Small things irritated, got on their nerves, water dripping from the leaking gutters, smoke in the kitchen and the smell of cabbage, the mess Gwyneth made getting ready to go to Brynllan. Damp washing and the old man hung by the front-room fire, and the morning papers did not arrive until early afternoon. The spread and turn of the pages made a draft of sound, filled the table space, filled the shabby room with Rhys and his reading.

"Oh God in heaven," said Enid. "Sick of it, I am. And all day yesterday it was the same, with you under my feet."

Rhys moved his feet out of the way of the broom. There were dog hairs all over the mat.

"Look at this place," Enid grumbled. "Not a chair to sit on. There's the coffee left out, the milk left out, and the floor is a dumping ground. Who hasn't put away my workbasket? And whose are those boots? Why must I be running around cleaning up after you all the time? Do you think I don't have enough to do?"

"What?" said Rhys.

It was mostly Gwyneth's. Her dirty tights were stuffed down the side of the armchair. Her cardigan was draped over it, her magazine under it. Lipstick, mascara, hair curlers, clips, brush and tissues were left on the cabinet. Her slippers were on the floor by the stove, her satchel on the floor by the cabinet, and the slop bucket needed emptying. Enid worked. Rhys was oblivious, hunting through the newspapers.

There was nothing. Nothing in the local paper of Mrs. Owen-Morgan being on the news. Nothing about anything having crashed except the prices on the stock exchange. And there had been nothing on last night's television either. Llanysted had regained its anonymity. Rhys frowned, went through a second time just to make sure, frowned again.

Enid was on her knees, raking the fire, but she stopped when she heard the silence behind her and looked at him. Ashes in the air had settled on her hair and there was a smudge on one cheek.

"What is it?"

"There's nothing in here," Rhys said.

"You haven't looked properly."

"I've looked twice."

"And there's nothing?"

"Not a mention."

"Why is that, then?"

Rhys leaned back. "It's been killed. Government intervention, I'd say. The story has been deliberately suppressed."

Enid settled on her heels. "Well now, that's queer, it is."

"It's significant."

"Don't we have a right to know what goes on? I thought it was a free press."

"It is," said Rhys. "But not when something's on the Official Secrets list. When it's Official Secrets no one has any rights. I was probably right then . . . it's either a brand-new guided missile or a Russian spy plane."

"And we'll never know," said Enid.

"No," said Rhys. "We'll never know."

Enid returned to the raking and Rhys started to tidy some of the things. He took the boots through to the scullery, and there in the dark corner by the woodpile was Blod. She did not move in welcome or love. Only her eyes touched him with all her suffering, watched him in her quiet, jailed patience. He wanted to tell her that what she pined for was gone, taken under the Official Secrets Act, and neither she nor he nor anyone else would ever know what it was. But Blod wouldn't understand words. She went on grieving and he closed the door on her and on his own dissatisfaction.

The slop bucket needed emptying. He took it to the outside drain. Captain Willoughby-Smythe was coming through the yard.

"Just the person I want to see."

"What about?" said Rhys.

"You're Rhys Williams, aren't you?"

"That's right."

"Can we go inside the house for a minute?"

Rhys shrugged and led the way.

Enid, who was washing the hearth, gave him a look of fury and rose from her knees. She wiped her soapy hands on her apron and quickly patted her hair. The smudge was still on her cheek. There was dried mud on her slacks and holes around the cuffs of her sweater and Rhys had allowed the English army captain to come in. Smoke hung in thin blue veils.

"You will forgive the mess, please," Enid murmured.

"I'm sorry to come barging in like this."

"I was in the middle of cleaning up."

"I just want a few words with your son."

"Sit down then. Would you like some tea?"

"If it's not too much trouble."

"It's no trouble," Enid said. "I could do with a cup."

Captain Willoughby-Smythe took a chair by the table. He opened a black briefcase full of papers, took out a small notebook and leafed through the pages. "Now," he said as the pen clicked, and he looked at Rhys and nodded. "A few questions, that's all."

They were vague, undirected questions that were strung together to form a statement. When the thing had struck, Rhys had been on this side of the mountain. No, he had not seen it, he had only gotten the impression that it was big, but he could not guess how big . . . the size of a jet plane perhaps? It had taken him, at a guess, a quarter of an hour to climb up and over the Mawrrhyn. He had searched down as far as the lake but he had seen and found nothing but shattered pieces of metal.

"You saw no person?" Captain Willoughby-Smythe asked.

Rhys looked surprised. "No. Should I have?"

"Not that I know of. I was asking you."

"You mean someone's alive? Someone was in it?"

"You saw someone?"

"No. And he'd have been dead anyway, wouldn't he?"

"Very probably. Did you pick anything up?"

"A few bits," said Rhys.

"Do you still have them?"

"Yes."

"Can I see?"

Rhys gave them to him. They lay on the spread palm of his hand, untarnished, mysterious, strangely beautiful, glowing dull in the light like lodestones. There was something about the pale silver metal, an attraction, as if it had once been part of something powerful and the power was still about it, forcing them to bend and stare until they could not look away.

Gently the army Captain examined them. Tensely, Rhys and Enid waited. Only the kettle boiling made them break away.

"So what was it then?" Enid asked.

"Hard to tell," said Captain Willoughby-Smythe.

"But you must have some idea."

"Maybe," he said cautiously as he gave the pieces back to Rhys.

"Meaning that you are not allowed to say?"

"No," he said. "Sorry and all that."

"Can I keep these?" Rhys asked.

"I don't see why not."

He made the last note, then the book snapped shut, was gone into his briefcase and locked away.

"Sugar?" Enid asked.

"Two, please," he said, and smiled.

It was strange how he changed, as if with the closing of the book he was no longer official, he could discard his military pose and relax. He became just an ordinary man watching Enid pour the tea, and the things he noticed were ordinary things . . . the roughened redness of her knuckles, the oldness of her clothes, the lines of worry around the corners of her mouth and eyes, the state of the kitchen, of the house . . . flagstone, rotten plaster, leaking gutters.

"A hard place, this," he said softly. "For a woman."

"Yes," said Enid. "It is, sometimes."

"How long have you been here now? Six months?"

"Five," said Enid.

"And your father?"

"He was born here . . . seventy-five years ago."

"Then he's too old to do much," the man murmured. "This place is going to decay. Remote, too. Was there nowhere else you could go?"

Enid stood very still.

"Who told you?"

"People talk," he said. "And finding out is part of my job."

"Excuse me," said Rhys. "I've got homework in the other room."

8

Gwyneth spent the afternoon watching Glyn Morris play football for Brynllan, standing on a cold touch-line seeing human shapes struggling through mud and fog after a dirty ball. It was not much fun. She had tea at his home but that was not much fun either. He had three younger brothers and a father who was big and beery, and the house had only one living room. Gwyneth stayed mostly in the kitchen with Mrs. Morris.

They talked about the old days when Mrs. Morris had lived in Llanysted, when she and Enid had been girls. They talked about the crash, and Mrs. Owen-Morgan on television, and how the police were out in Brynllan asking about a stranger. They talked about Mrs. Morris winning twenty-five pounds at bingo, how the quick-boiling ring on her new electric stove had broken, and however did Enid manage with all the inconvenience of that old place? Gwyneth had never really wondered how her mother managed, but talking about it helped pass the time until seven-thirty, when Glyn was taking her to the disco.

But at twenty-five past seven Glyn was watching a film on television and didn't want to go. He thought he might have a cold coming, and anyway Ifor Davis had gone away to Cardiff for the Easter weekend. Gwyneth said why couldn't they go without Ifor Davis, but Ifor had a car and Glyn said he didn't feel like walking, someone had kicked him on the shin and it hurt. So Gwyneth walked . . . to catch the bus home to Llanysted, and she was not friends with Glyn Morris anymore.

Rhys had no way of knowing she was coming home early, so he was not in the village to meet her. She had to walk alone up the long dark lane. Gwyneth had always been nervous of the dark. There were sounds which she could not identify. Sounds which seemed to close around her. A sudden breath and movement behind the field wall, a scream somewhere out in the thick silence of the mist. Gwyneth ran. Her heart was hammering against her ribs, her mind was in a panic, and her footsteps were loud and hollow on the lonely road. She seemed to attract the attention in the darkness that crept and followed and pounced.

"Stop it!"

But only she could stop it, the imaginings. She made herself stand and listen and face what she could not see. Slowly the night stabilized. There was nothing behind her. Only the soft sounds of cattle breathing, the stamp of their hooves on the hard ground, and the screech of a hunting owl. The mad hammering inside her grew quieter.

"Cows and owls," said Gwyneth. "How stupid you are!"

There was nothing to fear out here in these parts. There never was.

But once there had been a power.

Long ago, said Hywel Thomas, when the magic was alive in the hills of Wales, a young lord was crossing the mountains from Cwmvanwy. On the high moors by the Brechin he came across a woman gathering heather. "Can you tell me," he asked, "of any place where I can stay the night, for there is a wind in the clouds behind me, bringing in the snow, and I shall not reach home before dark." The woman smiled and told him to follow her. Her voice was wild and sweet, cold as water from the deep springs, piercing as starlight. And the young lord went with her.

He went with her through a door into the mountain, down into her halls under bog and stone. It was a land of fairy people, caverns of trees and flowers and fruits. And he stayed with the lady of the Mawrrhyn, forgetting his home and his loved ones and loving her.

But then he did remember, and he would stay no longer with her feasting and dancing, for there were others in the town expecting him and she must release him into his own world again. And so he rode into Caeravon thinking he was but two days late. But centuries had passed. The people of his land no longer knew him, and they were all dead, his wife and his children. He lived out his life alone in the crumbling castle, and the lady of the Mawrrhyn had no mercy on him.

In the darkness Gwyneth walked quietly, remembering the story.

They were funny, the people living hereabouts. They went to chapel every Sunday but they were not Christian. They believed in something older than that, powers that were deep and dark. They planted rowan by the door to keep away fey spirits, and they would not walk the moors at twilight or bring May blossom into the house. There were tales of the peat cutters hearing music under the mountains, and a strange fair-haired child who had shown Granny Hughes where the bilberries grew. And Hywel Thomas said the Mawrrhyn had a soul. They were funny people, believing in all that. But the dark living land was all around Gwyneth, the silence of earth and stone, and it was not hard to believe.

Then, faint and high up the valley, she heard a cry, and it was not magic. It tore through the legends with its human pain. A shot rang out, and another, and the silence dropped back but this time it was different. It was not wondering on supernatural things, it was knowing a person had been shot. Gwyneth was angry. For all the cruelty of the Mawrrhyn with her laws of dead sheep and rotting bog, she did not have human violence. But they were killing out there, the guns and the soldiers, and they had no law.

There was a light from the kitchen falling across the yard. Her mother and Rhys were standing there, staring upward, and there was shouting out on the hills.

"They've shot someone," Gwyneth said, panting.

"We heard," said Rhys.

"We ought to go and see."

"It's not our business," said Enid.

"But if they've shot someone . . ."

"We don't know they have."

"There was a cry."

"It might have been a rabbit," said Rhys.

"It was a person!" said Gwyneth. "And they can't just go around shooting people! We've got to do something!"

"It's not our business!" Enid repeated.

Hywell Thomas came out with his coat on.

"Shooting," he said.

"Yes," said Enid. "And it's over now."

"There's not much we *can* do," said Rhys.

"Shooting," said Hywel Thomas darkly. "And where is that bitch?"

"She was inside with you," said Rhys.

"She is not inside now," said Hywel Thomas.

"And you are not going looking for her in the dark and the fog," Enid said definitely. "She must take her own chances, and we are not interfering in army affairs."

On evenings and weekends they used the sitting room where the television was. Even after five months there was still a strange musty smell, an unlived-in feeling of faded photographs, red velour curtains, and dark polished furniture. The modern coffee table Enid had bought with green-shield stamps did not change it. It was still the room where Granny Thomas had died. A mausoleum. China dogs gathered dust on the mantelshelf and Gwyneth picked at the gold fringe of the cushion. The film on television was the same one Glyn had been watching.

"It sometimes helps to talk," Enid said.

"What about?" Gwyneth asked.

"Fallen out with Glyn Morris, haven't you?"

"How did you know?"

"Why else would you be home this time? Serious is it?"

Gwyneth shrugged. "I didn't like him much anyway."

"There you are then," said Enid. "Nothing to mope about. Plenty more there are at your age."

"Yes," said Gwyneth sourly. "Plenty there are . . . young men thick as grass out there on the mountains."

Enid watched her. It was not long since she had felt

the same, the loss and the bitterness and living here without hope. It was not easy to cope with an ending, and Gwyneth was young. Hard on her, it was, living here, accepting the isolation, the emptiness of days where she had no person. Enid knew how she felt.

The gold braid came free in a long curling thread.

"It's always the same here," Gwyneth said. "Nothing ever happens."

"What do you mean?" said Rhys. "It's all been happening."

"Like what?"

"All this excitement."

"A bang and a couple of shots," said Gwyneth.

"How much more do you want?"

"Nothing's changed, has it?" said Gwyneth. "It's still the same as it always was . . . fog, and mountains, and us living here. It hasn't touched us in any way. Even Brynllan is better than here. At least they're keeping the interest alive. At least the police are around asking."

"Asking what?"

"Questions."

"What about?"

"They're doing a house-to-house. Looking for a stranger."

"Well, that's silly for a kickoff."

"Why is it silly? It shows they're awake."

"No one could have gotten out of that alive," said Rhys.

"Who said it was anything to do with that?"

"You did."

"I never. I was simply telling you what Mrs. Morris told me."

"Looking for a stranger, you said."

"But I never said what stranger."

"You implied."

"For all I know, they could be looking for a mur-
derer."

"We'd have heard."

"So all right!" Gwyneth said angrily. "It's silly! And
I didn't ask for your opinion! All I'm saying is that
the interest is alive, which is better than sitting on your
fat backside watching that junk!"

"Must you talk to your brother like that?" Enid
asked.

"I'm not her brother," said Rhys. "I'm a stand-in
for Glyn Morris, and I reckon he had a lucky escape."

9

Enid had gone to bed when the grandfather clock churred and struck eleven. In the front room the fire had burned low and they were playing cards for matches . . . Rhys and Gwyneth and the old man. Blod whined in the outside darkness. She had been whining on and off for an hour or more. They would hear her scrabbling at the front door. Then she would disappear for a while, return some time later, and whine again. No one went to let her in. It would teach her, thought Rhys, to go boning off. Maybe she would learn to behave herself now that she was shut out to cry for him under the walls and the windows.

He would not answer her, but she was not easy to ignore.

"Will you see to that dog!" Enid called down.

"That was Mom," said Gwyneth.

"I heard."

"Better see to her then, hadn't you?"

He would not see to her yet. He had a straight flush and the old man was rubbing his hands with three tens and a pair of aces. They could both sense battle to the death and they would not leave it. Rhys raised ten matches. Hywel Thomas followed and Gwyneth could either throw in her hand or risk losing everything. But Blod was on the porch, her claws scratching hard on the wood and stone, her whining shrill and insistent.

"Will you see to that dog!" Enid shouted.

"Blast!" said Rhys and flung down his cards.

"How can I sleep with her carrying on?"

"If either of you look at my cards . . ."

"We won't," Gwyneth said sweetly.

But he knew they would . . . both of them . . . cheat. And Enid was moving around upstairs, about to come down. Rhys put the cards in his pocket and went through to the hall. The door, swollen with damp, jammed on the flagstones, made a white scratch mark as he heaved it open. The light fled outward, glittered yellow on fog and drizzle, glittered on Blod's eyes. She stood away from him at the edge of the darkness. She did not offer to come in.

"Flaming well come on, will you!" Rhys said.

Enid came down in her dressing gown. "What is it?"

"The damn thing won't come."

"Blod!" said Enid.

"Blod!" roared Hywel Thomas. "You come on in here!"

She would not come.

Her tail wagged slightly and she cried in her soft doggy voice. She was telling them . . . it was out there beyond the yards, strong as a sheep call, and she couldn't leave it. She wanted them to come. Her eyes were dark and troubled. She was acting out her distress but they would not understand her. The cold was seeping into the house and the old man came to tell her.

"In here, you fleabag you!"

Blod whined.

She was cowed but she was not obeying even Hywel Thomas. She turned sadly away and was gone into the night.

"Well!" said Enid. "Disobedient, she is!"

"She's never been like this before," said Rhys.

"Aye," said Hywel Thomas. "She has the sensing."

"She has no sense!" said Enid.

"All is not right with her somewhere."

"You mean something is out there?" Enid asked.

"She is not easy, see? She has the knowing. I will get my coat."

"I suppose you forgot to lock the fowl house," Enid said to Rhys.

"I never."

"You will put your coat on and see, please."

"I locked it!"

"You are not letting your grandfather go out at this time of night."

"But Mom!"

"If you please," said Enid. 'We shall be having no sleep at all if she carries on like this."

Animals sensed things, but Rhys sensed nothing out there in the dark and damp, only the raw cold making his teeth ache and his nose run, and it was cards he had in his pocket and no handkerchief. The mist was lifting. He could feel the mountains rising dark beyond black buildings, and the flashlight was pale and pathetic. The fowl houses were padlocked, the shed where they kept the sheep feed was bolted, and there was nothing around the yard and outbuildings. Nothing but whisps of white mist and his own breath curling. He was about to go back in when he saw Blod by the paddock gate, her eyes watching him. The silence between them was very sharp and still and the darkness spread and waited.

"I'm going to kill you, Blod," Rhys said.

She did not move or answer him, merely watched, a gaze that was firm and steady, leveling with him. She had not come for his hate or love, she had come because she still hoped he would listen. This was the last chance Blod would give him, and he knew by her look that there was an ending between them if he failed. It was not she who would give way.

"Go on then," Rhys said. "And you'd better make sure the explanation is a good one. And if it's mountains you're after, the answer is still no."

She whined, the soft wordless telling of Blod to him. And it was not mountains.

It was across the paddock he had to go. Rhys turned up his collar and followed her, and she stayed a few paces ahead, now and then glancing back to make sure of him. He did not question her in the cold sound of the stream, the song of the black water that filled the night. He knew now Blod had something and he would wade the stream if he had to. But he did not have to. Blod went toward the barn.

The barn was not used. It was old and broken down and filled with the junk of decades. His flashlight beam lit on stone walls and arrow-slit windows and a roof that was partly open to the sky. Not much shelter there, but into it Blod had gone. Rhys stood in the doorway, in the dark scent of musty hay. An owl flew over him with a whir of wings and a quick screech of alarm.

"Blod?" said Rhys. "You in here?"

His light lurched around the walls, making great bat-winged shadows. Picked at the outline of things . . . a broken-down tractor, pitchforks, chaffcutters, feeding troughs, and piles of sacks. He trod softly over old straw and baling twine, his eyes raking the dark places. And he saw the shine of Blod's eyes through the spokes of a buck rake. She was guarding something that lay huddled in the corner. Not a sheep.

"What is it?" Rhys said.

She cried to him.

"What is it then?"

He had to move the rusty milk churns to reach her.

"What have you found, Blod?"

Rhys squeezed through the gap and shone the flashlight.

"Oh, my God!"

10

The boy was maybe younger than Rhys. His face was blanched white, stricken, and there was terror in his eyes, blue terror shot with pain. Never before had Rhys seen anything like it. He was covered with blood. Everywhere, blood. Matted in his blond hair, on his face and clothes, dark among the filth and the wetness. Blood seeping scarlet in the flashlight.

"Oh, God," said Rhys. "What have you done!"

He squatted and the boy cringed against the wall, mute and shivering. His pale lips were moving slightly but no sound came. There was just the terror staring, fear of someone who did not know Rhys, who expected violence, more violence, more hurt. It was not human fear, it was fear of something wild and trapped and terribly wounded. And Rhys was bound to hurt him. He had to hurt in order to help him, and he himself was appalled and frightened.

Only Blod had no fear. She licked him gently, her warmth on his cold and broken skin. She cleaned and cried and cared for his hurt. And Rhys saw his fingers moving in her fur as if he must touch and hold the only thing to comfort him. He suddenly clutched her and the movement caused the blood to flow, freshly welling through the soaked front of his shirt. There was no time for Rhys to stay useless. He jammed the flashlight in the buck rake and angled it down. Gently he reached for the boy.

"It's all right. I'm not going to hurt."

The blue eyes were on him. The fear pitched.

"You know what I'm saying?" Rhys asked. "I'm not going to hurt you. Animals know who to trust. She wouldn't have come for me if she thought I would hurt. So you got to trust me too."

There was no more resistance.

Rhys undid the small pearl buttons, pulled the shirt away. It was ghastly. Deep and dark with congealed blood was a huge wound in the flesh below the boy's shoulder, as if a metal fist had smashed through the skin and entered his body. Small runnels of blood crept from the torn edges, trickled and ran.

"Bloody hell," Rhys muttered.

He didn't know what to do. He could only stare, useless.

And the boy was watching him.

"They shot you, didn't they?"

The pale lips moved. "Yes."

"The mindless bastards!"

"They didn't know what they did."

"Christ on the cross said that. Can you walk?"

"Not yet."

"I'll have to carry you then."

"If you will just leave me . . ."

"You're likely to bleed to death."

"I have to get away from here."

"I know. Later, Let's see to you first. Move out of the way, Blod."

The boy's eyes closed in defeat, giving up. Rhys kicked aside churns and sacks and clutter. He would have to drag him to the open space, drag him because there was no other way. And with every move Rhys knew he was hurting, maybe killing. But he had learned with the sheep that day on the mountain that the body had to bear, and it was not his law. But the blood was on his hands when he went back for the flashlight, and Blod was grieving. He's dead, thought Rhys. But he was afraid to find out. The last light lingered on the boy's drained face and snapped out into darkness.

It was magic.

A breath of wind whispered through the fir plantation. There was music in the midnight stream. And the boy's skin gave out a pale waxed light, as if he were luminous. Rhys looked up. The mist had gone. Through the roof space he could see the sky and the stars burning down on him. Stars like eyes, watching and listening.

"God," said Rhys. "Don't let him be dead."

The boy was not dead.

He groaned when Rhys went to lift him and the pain was a sign of his living.

"Where are you taking me?"

"Home."

"Don't let them find me."

"No, all right."

"Don't let them take me."

"I'm not. I'm taking you to Mom."

Rhys carried him. He was light, almost weightless, pale in the starlight, his face reflecting the shine. But after a while he was heavy, hurting as Rhys moved and his mind would not let go. Over and over he was murmuring the same words . . . Don't let them take me, please don't let them take me . . . like it was a prayer. And over and over Rhys soothed him with promises which he did not hear or did not believe, so he kept on asking . . . Don't let them take me, please.

Then quite suddenly he did let go, and he was not knowing pain anymore, only rest and unconsciousness, and Rhys was making promises to no one. Fear grabbed his guts as he struggled through the poached ground between the stone gateposts. The boy was gone. His head lolled backward and Rhys was praying again.

"Please, God, don't let him die on me."

There was no answer, only the silence of stars and mountains, and Blod whining, telling him to hurry. But he could not hurry because his feet sank in the mud and his whole body was tense and aching with the strain. The yard stretched before him a mile long.

"Mom!" Rhys screamed.

She was inside the house and did not hear him. The door was shut and the radio going. He had to hammer with his bootheel.

"Mom! Let me in! Quick!"

It was Gwyneth who opened the door.

Rhys almost fell into the light, with Blod under his feet. He trod on her paw and she yelped and the room was full of a chaos of things, people who were suddenly made electric with the emergency. Gwyneth rushed to clear the table. Enid filled the kettle, raked the fire for heating the water, sent Gwyneth to fetch sheets for bandaging and some clean towels. Blod fled to a safe place behind the easy chair, and all the time Rhys was standing there holding the boy.

"Put him here now," said Hywel Thomas.

He took the weight off his shoulders and they laid him on the bare table.

"Kindling," said Enid.

She rammed small pieces of sticks between the fire bars. Gwyneth brought the sheets and towels, found disinfectant and a bowl. Then there was nothing to do but wait for the water. Rhys leaned against the door. He felt weak and shaking. And they were staring down at the boy in the brightness, at the pallor of his face, the extent of his wound, and his strange unearthly appearance.

"Oh, Mom," said Gwyneth. "He is beautiful!"

"Aye," said Hywel Thomas grimly. "Beauty it is, but not of this world. He doesn't belong to our kind."

"He is terribly hurt," said Enid.

"Shot," said Gwyneth. "They shot him!"

"I'll get my coat," said Enid.

"What for?"

"To fetch the ambulance."

"You can't do that, Mom!" Gwyneth shrilled.

And Rhys was against the door, barring her way.

"You can't do that, Mom."

Enid stared. "He is hurt too much for us! We have to do something!"

She looked to the old man for support but it was not there. They were all against her. And the boy lay pale and bleeding, and the kettle started to sing.

"He needs help!" Enid shouted. "What's the matter with you all?"

"He is not needing help with an ambulance," Hywel Thomas said.

"We can't turn him over to the authorities, Mom," said Gwyneth.

"He is not one of us," said Hywel Thomas.

"Then who is he?" Enid snapped.

"He is hers."

"Whose?"

"Mawrrhyn. He has the fairness."

"Don't talk nonsense!"

"He came from the mountain. I am telling you that."

"From the plane, Mom," said Rhys.

"The one they're all looking for," said Gwyneth.

"And he is hurt bad, needing . . ."

"No!" said Gwyneth. "No! You can't do that! You can't give him to doctors and hospitals. Don't you see? They're hunting him! You can't hand him over. They've already shot him once. We've got to keep him here. We've got to help him ourselves. . . ."

"And if he dies?" Enid asked. "If he dies here with us?"

"He won't," said Gwyneth. "We won't let him. That water's hot. Pass me the cotton wool."

Hywel Thomas knew how to heal sick creatures. A lifetime had taught him, hardened the hands that must hurt to be kind. He did not flinch when he dug out the bullet. It was just something that had to be done, doctoring, like sheep with the maggots. He treated the wound with ointment he used for the sheep and Gwyneth did the bandaging. The boy did not regain consciousness, and they did not try moving him upstairs but put him on the sitting-room sofa. Rhys banked up the fire for the night. They could do nothing more for him.

Only pray.

Enid was right. He needed a hospital. Blood transfusions, X rays, proper doctors. He could have a fractured skull. He could have a broken rib. There was no way Gwyneth could tell. No way the old man could tell either.

Gwyneth stood looking down at him.

A gold-white boy.

He was clean now, all of him washed, his fair hair spread damp on the pillow. He was wearing one of Granny Thomas' flannelette nightgowns because Rhys had no spare pajamas. Beautiful, thought Gwyneth. She had never seen anyone so beautiful and she would not leave him. She would spend the night in the armchair in case he should wake and need her. And Blod would not leave him either. She would sleep on the mat beside him with her head on her paws. They were watching together, she and Blod.

She tucked a blanket around the boy.

"Don't die in this night," Gwyneth said softly.

It was wasting her feelings. He could not hear or know. With one last look at him, she switched off the light. It was weird, or maybe it was wonderful. Gwyneth did not know which. There was a light to him, white and pale and burning, like a halo about his head. She could see his features quite clearly, each separate curl of his hair faintly shining. She stood and stared at him without moving for a long time. The room was flickering with fire shadows but the light of the boy was strange and steady, and the power of him seemed to touch her deep down inside.

And sitting in the chair with the blanket around her, she could not tear her eyes away from him or think of sleeping. But she did sleep, because she woke quite suddenly and it was early morning. There was a gold light shining through the threadbare curtains and the fire had burned down. She didn't know why she had woken. The house was quiet and the boy was lying still, just as she had last seen him. But Blod was sitting upright by his side, staring at his face as if she was expecting something to happen. Gwyneth went softly and quickly to the window and drew back the curtain.

Morning.

A great gold miracle. The sun was shining. Brightness everywhere, over the paddock and the fir woods and the slopes of the Brechin. The whole world was green and yellow and sparkling, glinting with water drops. There were daffodils in bloom, a hint of new green over the larch trees, and a pair of titmice swung on a string of fat they had hung from the bare branches of the rowan tree. The brilliance was charged with a feeling close to joy, things rising from the dead . . . Easter Sunday! Gwyneth wanted to leap about, fling open doors and windows, sing and shout. But she stood still in the magic. Something behind her was stronger than all that. Slowly Gwyneth turned around.

The boy was watching her. Eyes that were blue as the outside sky fixed on her face.

He did not speak to her. He just watched. And Blod pushed her nose against his neck, wanting his attention. But he was seeing nothing else in the room but Gwyneth. The light of him was gone in the daylight. His strangeness was more ordinary. His face was drawn and colorless. But the power was still in him. Power in the silence between them, and Gwyneth did not know what to say. She spread her hands.

"It is a lovely day for the time of year."

She was a girl speaking to him out of sunlight, and he did not know her.

"How are you feeling?"

"Where am I?" he asked weakly.

"High Valley Farm, Llanysted," Gwyneth said. "In Wales."

It meant nothing to him.

"Wales," said Gwyneth. "By England. You know?"

He did not know.

He did not know the girl or the place, or how he came to be there or why. The last he remembered was cold and pain and terror, a boy and a dog and a dark barn. Gwyneth came nearer to him, watching his eyes for signs of amnesia. He'd had a bang on his head but the blueness was not blank. Down inside, he was struggling to understand.

Gwyneth squatted beside him. "It might be better not to try."

But he had to try. It was important.

"Who are you?"

"Gwyneth."

"I don't remember you."

"You were not noticing much when Rhys brought you."

"I don't remember you or this place."

"You remember Blod, though, don't you?"

"Blod?"

"The dog," said Gwyneth. "It was she who found you."

"Blod," he said softly. "Is that her name?"

"She is here," said Gwyneth.

He turned his head.

Blod . . . dog eyes looking deeply into his own. He did not forget her. He smiled as he reached for here. He knew what he had to thank Blod for . . . his life. Her blind, unquestionable animal sense had brought help for him, had trusted him into the warmth and safety of this house, and trusted him now to the girl.

He closed his eyes. It was not that easy. The trust of people was not blind and instinctive like the trust of a dog. And he could not lie here helpless, trusting the girl with his life. His life was not her responsibility. His freedom was not her problem.

"I have to go," he said quietly.

"Oh no you don't."

Gwyneth was quick. He was not walking out into that bright morning and being shot down by soldiers. He was not going anywhere in Granny Thomas' flannelette nightgown. She held him down by his shoulders and he had no strength to fight her. He was weakened by the loss of blood. Pinned by her hands and the tone of her voice.

"You will lie still, please, and do as you are told."

He stared up at her. He did not struggle.

"You don't understand."

"I do. To move will start up the bleeding."

"I can't go on lying here."

"Well, you're not leaving, so you may as well get used to it."

"You don't understand. They will be coming for me."

Gwyneth released him, glanced at the door.

Nervous.

"Who?" Gwyneth asked.

"The men with guns."

"Is that all? You don't need to worry about them. They don't know you're here and we're not going to tell them."

"They will come," he said. "They will find me. Dead or alive they will find me."

"No, they won't."

He sighed.

"Listen to me," he said wearily. "They will have to find me. . . . They know what I am, you see, and they daren't let me stay loose. I have knowledge and they want it. They want *me*. And they will take me . . . into their custody. I have to get away from here. I have to get away now, before they come. So will you give me my clothes . . ."

"Don't be stupid!"

"Please . . . Gwyneth."

Gwyneth moved and did not answer him. She stirred the ashes of the fire and held her hands to the small warmth. Knowledge, he said. And the morning was not bright and gold anymore. She didn't know what to do. She glanced at the boy. His eyes were closed again. He was pale and patient and waiting for her. His fingers dug into Blod's fur. He couldn't go. Whatever he said, whatever he'd done . . . he couldn't go. He wasn't meant to be shot and captured, grilled for his knowledge in a government jail. He was too beautiful. . . .

"What have you done?" Gwyneth asked quietly. "Spying is it?"

"It was a routine observation flight," he said.

"Spying," said Gwyneth. "Where d'you come from? Slav, are you, with your blond hair? Russian? What's your name?"

He opened his eyes to look at her.

The house was very still.

Hers, Hywel Thomas had said.

"My name is Erlich," he said. "I come from Eridani Epsilon."

"Where?" said Gwyneth.

"Eridani Epsilon. Eleven light-years away across space."

12

"I don't believe it," said Rhys.

"I'm telling you," said Gwyneth.

"You've got to be off your head!"

"It's true," said Gwyneth. "Look at him!"

Look at him. . . .

Erlich, with his pale power, sleeping . . . not of this world.

"He was probably raving," said Rhys.

"He was perfectly sane," said Gwyneth.

Rhys clenched his fists.

In the clear light of morning, the boy had not lied.

"Have you thought what it means?" Rhys asked softly.

"Yes," said Gwyneth. "Most of it."

Rhys turned away.

Not one of us, the old man had said. But he was not a lord from the mountain halls, he was a star lord, come with his ship to this earth. It was up there now, a flying saucer, dull silver fragments scattered over the slopes of the Mawrrhyn. And the soldiers were up there. Earlier on, Rhys had heard them go by, the army trucks rumbling along the lane, up the long track by the Brechin. There was no mist to hinder them now. It was all bright and open, everything clear. From the window, he could see men with binoculars positioned on the high points. He saw a helicopter skim the ridges. He saw the sunlight flashing. The reality of it all came crashing into him.

They knew what that thing was. They knew it was manned. They had to kill that story. If news of it had leaked out, it would have started a worldwide panic . . . great black headlines of UFOs, space invaders, and the threat to international security. They would have to find Erlich too, keep his presence dark. It was more than their lives were worth to let him escape. That was a superpower lying there on Hywel Thomas' sofa, worse than guns or missiles or atom bombs, more dangerous than any communist army.

Rhys turned back to the room and stared at him.

He was only a boy. Only a boy, who could travel the universe at speeds beyond the speed of light, who had power enough and knowledge enough to blast this earth to a cinder. But Rhys could see nothing on that sleeping face, no trace of the mean, oppressive instincts given to men. Erlich was no conqueror. Nor was he meant to be captured and contained in some Ministry of Defense prison. Not meant to be bled by greedy governments, tapped of his knowledge, used and abused and desecrated. He was meant to be out there, among the stars from where he came. And Rhys had already made a promise.

"We're not handing him over."

"No," said Gwyneth.

"What'll we do, though?"

"I don't know."

"There's got to be something," Rhys said. "Some way."

"Maybe his own people will come and take him home," said Gwyneth.

"If they make it in time."

"If we can keep him safe long enough," said Gwyneth.

A log slipped on the fire.

"I don't think we should tell Mom," said Gwyneth.

"Not tell me what?" Enid said.

She had come down late.

It was ten-thirty. Rhys and Gwyneth had been up for hours, and the old man had taken Blod to Hughes Farm for the milk. Enid was met by an empty kitchen full of last night's mess. The meat was not in the oven, the pastry was not made, and the remains of breakfast were still on the table. All the work and the lateness seemed to shriek at her from the bright Sunday morning, and she must see first to the injured boy. But they had cared for him, Rhys and Gwyneth. She had crept on them quietly in the sitting room, which was the only tidy room in the house. The hearth was washed, the fire was freshly burning, and there was a bowl of daffodils on the polished table. But she had not come to worship, it was only briefly that she could stay with her concern.

"How is he?"

"He is no worse," said Gwyneth.

Enid sat by him, rested a cool hand on his forehead.

"He is no better either," said Enid.

"Grandad was happy enough."

"Your grandfather does not know. Have you let the fowls out?"

"Yes," said Rhys.

"You will be fetching Dr. Price-Jones this morning?"

"No."

"How long is he to lie here unconscious then?"

"He needs rest, Mom," said Gwyneth.

"He needs other things besides rest. Treatment and nourishment."

Enid pulled down the blanket, opened the nightshirt. The first traces of blood were through the bandage.

"What is it you are not telling me?" Enid asked.

They looked at each other as if it were something grave and important. Enid waited but she did not watch them. They must decide for themselves in the silence.

She touched the pale cheek of the boy. "What did they do to you, my lovely?"

Precious he was, and he would not lie there and die if it was in her power to bring help to him. She would go for Dr. Price-Jones herself, and it did not matter what they were not telling her. She would go now. The work and the dinner were not important. A Land-Rover pulled into the yard. Dafydd Jones, Enid thought.

"Willoughby-blasted-what's-it!" said Rhys.

"What'll we do?" Gwyneth asked.

"Mom," said Rhys.

"Yes, what is it?"

"You got to go out there and stop him coming in here."

Enid looked at him, stung. "Who are you giving orders to, boy?"

"Oh, Mom," said Gwyneth. "Don't take it like that. There's not time!"

It was terrible and urgent.

The door of the Land-Rover banged. There were voices and Enid was watching Rhys.

"You've got to listen, Mom."

"I've *got* to do nothing."

"He woke up earlier on," said Gwyneth.

"Who did?"

"Erlich."

Enid looked down at him.

"This is Erlich?"

"He told me," said Gwyneth. "His name is Erlich. And Grandad was right: He's not one of us. It's like there really are fairy folk living under the Mawrrhyn. . . . He's not hers . . . but he's not of our world either. Look at him, Mom. You can see, can't you? You can see he's different."

He was different, right from the beginning.

Precious, Enid thought.

"He has powers," said Gwyneth. "And knowledge we don't have. We've got to help him Mom. We can't let them take him. We can't let him be robbed of his knowledge. He's got to get back to his own kind, back to his own world. Please, Mom."

The words trickled into Enid's mind without any meaning. Believing and disbelieving, she understood and did not understand. It was too much to take in and there was no time to think or to question.

"I never meant to order you," Rhys said. "But he's done nothing. Don't take it out on him, please, Mom."

A knock came on the door.

She must lie or seduce, anything to keep the English army captain from knowing about the boy. There was no need for Gwyneth to beg or Rhys to apologize. She would do it anyway. Rhys watched the stillness of her face and did not know her thoughts. He turned from her and his lips were bitter.

"I'll go," he said dully.

"There is no need," said Enid.

"Oh, Mom," said Gwyneth in relief. "You'll do it?"

"He will believe things better coming from me."

Enid had not come downstairs prepared for a confrontation. Her hair was not combed and she was not wearing shoes or slippers because she had left her tights drying over the stove. Rhys and Gwyneth were shut in the room with the boy and she was alone in the dark hallway. Knock, knock, knock. Captain Willoughby-Smythe was demanding and she must answer him. For a few quick seconds Enid breathed in the calm.

He was watching the play of cloud and sunlight over the hills. Tall as the mountain he was, and behind him the Mawrrhyn squatted, the shape of her sharp and menacing against the brightness of the sky. He turned when he heard the door open and his eyes were a quiet gray-blue. He smiled when she saw her.

"I was getting dressed," Enid explained.

"Sorry," he said. "I didn't think."

"We were late going to bed, see. What is it you are wanting?"

"A word with Rhys again, if possible."

"I'm not sure he is around."

"A word with you, then."

"What about?"

"Can I come in?" .

"It is lovely out here in the sunshine."

"No tea then?"

Enid hesitated. Keep him out, Rhys had ordered. But if she did, he would wonder why. "Come in," Enid said. She turned and led him through to the kitchen. "You will excuse the mess please. I have not had time to clear up."

The kitchen smelled strongly of disinfectant. There was a white shirt soaking in a bucket of blood-red water. Enid moved it to the scullery and filled the kettle. A torn sheet was draped over the back of the chair. She moved that too. The army captain stood, watching her, immaculate in his uniform, the creases in his trousers sharp as knife edges. And she, with her bare legs, padded through the mess, aware of him, aware that he was noticing. There was a bowl of bread and milk gone cold on the table, and a small bottle of medicinal brandy by the cornflakes.

"He is not eating," Enid said.

"The old man?"

"He has the cough bad on his chest, see."

"I passed him," said the captain. "Along the road with the dog."

Enid frowned.

"It's no good telling him. What is it about, this word you want?"

He had something rolled under his arm, a bundle wrapped in plastic. Something that fell and glittered when he shook it free. It was a silver suit, torn and mud stained, weightless and beautiful. She thought it was made of beaten metal, shimmering and engraved with patterns. But it was soft when she touched it and he told her it was synthetic fiber.

"It is beautiful," said Enid.

"Incredibly beautiful."

"The work of it. Where did you find it?"

"The helicopter spotted it. In the reeds by the lake."

"What was it doing there?"

"Obviously someone discarded it."

"But why?"

"I guess because someone did not want to be seen," said Captain Willoughby-Smythe. "This fabric not only reflects light like a mirror, it is also luminous. In the dark it is even more beautiful. It glows like a silver beacon. And that's why I wanted Rhys. He said he searched around the lake."

"And you think he saw this thing?"

"Maybe."

"If he did he would have said."

"Unless he was afraid to say."

Enid stared.

"Why should he be afraid?"

There was something the man was about to tell her. He was thoughtful and quiet and not quite knowing how. He was bound by his job to secrecy, but there was something he wanted her to know, because he was concerned, because maybe he was afraid for her. He took a few quick turns along the mat and then stopped.

"We think there is a person at large, Mrs. Williams."

"You mean someone got out of that crashed plane alive?"

"Possibly."

"And you're worried?"

"Last night someone was seen at the head of the valley, not far from here. I don't want to alarm you, but this farm is one of the nearest houses, and he could be armed and dangerous."

"You are telling me to be careful?" Enid said softly.

"Yes I am going to give you a phone number."

"There is a phone at the next farm."

"If there is anything . . . if you have any cause at all . . . call me. Call this number and mention my name. Don't take any chances."

"I see"

He gave her a folded piece of paper, watched as she placed it carefully behind the clock. Then he smiled.

"It's bank holiday. Are you going out today?"

"Not that I know of," Enid said.

"Do you ever go out?"

"I work in Brynllan three days a week."

"I mean to enjoy yourself?"

"Around here?"

"Maybe when all this is over . . ."

"Excuse me," said Enid. "The kettle's boiling."

13

The evening was fine and golden, spreading brilliance down the valley. But the sun was low over the Mawr-rhyn and the farmhouse was dark in her shadow. It was the shadow that Enid must be free of, the feeling of bondage. She must go for help, but they would not let her, Rhys and Gwyneth and the old man. All through the day they would not let her. Now they were watching her uneasily as she checked her purse for change for the collection plate and pulled on her gloves.

"Don't forget to shut the fowls up."

"This is stupid!" said Gwyneth.

"Why is it stupid?" Enid asked.

"You haven't been to chapel since Christmas."

"And now it's Easter," Enid said coolly. "So I'm going again."

"But why? Why are you going? You never bother other times."

Enid looked at her coldly.

"I will tell you why I am going," she said. "I am going for him, because you will do nothing. I am going to pray for him and I refuse to be kept a prisoner in my own home. Does that satisfy you?"

"Mom," Rhys said softly and warningly. "If you are planning . . ."

Enid's eyes flashed angrily.

"This is between me and God!" she said bitterly. "At least you will allow me that much!"

He did not believe her. His knuckles were white, gripping the back of the chair. Enid stood quietly in the mean room in her navy suit and white hat. It had never been like this before between her and Rhys. Never so grim, and hostile, and untrusting. There was a force in his eyes that would not give way to her. She thought perhaps he would physically try to stop her.

"Let her go, boyo," said Hywel Thomas.

"You know what she intends to do!"

"Aye, but she has the conscience, same as us."

"Mom wouldn't hurt him," Gwyneth said.

"You heard her! Between her and God, she said. Between her and God and the telephone, more like!"

"You will let me pass, please," Enid said.

For a few seconds more he held her, then stood aside.

She walked past him, out into the evening, and it was not fresh air and freedom she found. It was cold in the thin suit and she had left her hymn book on the table but she was not going back for it. Rhys was in the doorway, watching her. She knew he was watching her without looking around. She could feel his gaze hard and sharp as a claw, raking her. He would hate her and not forgive. She wanted to lash out at him, scream that he was making her do this and she had no choice. But she made herself walk, quietly and efficiently, and her back view gave nothing away.

The heels of her shoes tapped briskly on the hard surface of the road. Shadows lay long across the evening fields. And high in the empty sky an airplane left a white trail and the sound came screaming. She was running then because she could not bear the memory or the knowledge. It had crashed all those days ago but he was still there, the hurt boy. She could not bear the tragedy of his young white face, the long slow sleep of his dying.

They were stupid, Rhys and Gwyneth, not listening to reason. And Hywel Thomas was a silly old man believing in fairies and herb magic. It was human help Erlich needed. Human help he was going to have. She heard a vehicle coming behind her, the shrill hoot of a horn, and she sidestepped hurriedly into wet grass and primroses, cursing the delay, willing it to hurry. But it did not hurry. It slowed and stopped . . . a Land-Rover, army khaki. And the chapel bell was ringing.

"A lift, Mrs. Williams?"

Captain Willoughby-Smythe, Ministry of Defense. It seemed she could not escape him.

And she did not want to escape. Her shoes were pinching and it was a long way she had to walk. It was warm inside, smelling of diesel, almost cozy. She was not alone anymore, and she had noticed before how nice he looked when he smiled.

"You're going somewhere in a hurry?"

"Chapel," said Enid.

He wiped the dust from the dashboard clock. "Six-twenty-five. That's cutting it fine."

He slid the Land-Rover into gear and drove on. She studied his face, the firm line of his jaw, the

pleasant creases around his eyes. He was not an auto-
maton, a piece of army equipment. He was a human
person with a human capacity for understanding. He
would take away her terrible responsibility if she let
him. He would take away Erlich. But Enid knew what
would happen if she told Captain Willoughby-Smythe.
Rhys would hate her then for sure.

The man glanced at her.

"Is something worrying you?"

"I just wish it was over," Enid said.

"What?"

"The hunting and the capture," she said.

"It will be soon. We'll find him."

"She is very cruel," Enid murmured.

"Who?" he asked curiously.

"The mountain," said Enid.

"What makes you say that?"

"I feel her. She will make us pay for this, every one
of us."

Again he glanced at her. He did not laugh.

"Perhaps I should not have told you," he said
grimly.

It was good being with him, comforting, but it was
too short, the distance to the end of the lane. She
wanted him to go on driving, take her anywhere away
from there. Or at the last minute turn to him and
say . . . Take me to Caeravon, I need a doctor. Then
he would ask why and she would tell him and the
worrying would be over. But she had to thank him for
the ride, smile at him and close the door and watch
him drive the other way, toward Brynllan. Police in a
parked car made notes of her. Enid went toward the
chapel.

The people were coming, the men of the mountain
farms, the women of Llanysted, coming to the chapel
for the evening service, gathering outside in small

groups as if they were waiting for someone. Enid
glanced behind her. There was no one on the road. Yet
they were waiting. She stopped still, suddenly knowing
. . . they were waiting for her. And the shadow of the
Mawrrhyn crept cold down the valley.

They knew something . . . concerning her.

She saw the knowledge in their faces, caught it in
the scraps of their murmuring.

"She is coming, then."

"The poor thing."

"After all her other trouble."

"She is not knowing what else to do."

"And will it help? The praying?"

She had to walk through them, the eyes and the
people.

"Enid."

Enid nodded. "Evening, Mrs. Owen-Morgan. Mr.
Price. Evening, Mrs. Hughes."

The chapel door was open and the organ was softly
playing. She had a glimpse of richness, of brown wood
and daffodils, but she would not go in. She would not
go with the women in Sunday hats and the men in
dark suits for the praying and singing. She would not
kneel in the undercurrents of their other faith that
flowed out to the sky and the mountains, acknowledging
a different power, worshiping a different holiness. She
was not part of their mystery. She did not believe like
they did, only that Erlich was hurt and she must help
him.

"You go in, Enid," they said.

"Peace for your mind, see?"

"Be all right with us, you will."

"You let us do the caring."

But it didn't work like that. There was an old ruling.
The power chose its own servants and Enid must carry
it alone. They could not help with their compassion,

could not share or take the weight away. She pushed through them.

"You will excuse me, please," she said.

And they let her go, walking down the open road to Caeravon.

"The poor dear," said the voices, fading.

"There's a state she is in."

"Where is she going?"

She did not go far. A red car drew alongside her and the door opened.

"Caeravon, is it?" said Dafydd Jones.

"I can quite easily walk," said Enid.

"And I can quite easily take you. Get in."

"You will miss the service."

"It doesn't matter. Get in."

She sat alongside him, the gnarled man who had planted the fir trees by the Brechin. She did not ask him what he knew or how. People around here had strange ways of knowing, like it was born in them, deep and instinctive. Like the earth conveyed knowledge or the Mawrrhyn herself whispered through the sleeping villages. They knew every grass blade and berry, every stone. Who loved on Saturday nights in Hugh Griffith's barn. Why Wynn Evans would not speak to Dafydd Price. When the road over the high moors had been made. But it was never spoken of directly, this knowledge of theirs. It did not come from one to another in the gossip. It came hidden beneath other things. It was hidden now between Enid and Dafydd Jones.

"Is it Dr. Price-Jones you are wanting?"

"If you please," said Enid.

"The old man, is it?"

"He has the cough."

"Been a bad winter for the cough."

"Damp," said Enid.

"Aye."

It was three miles to Caeravon into the sunset and the Mawrrhyn swung away into dark. And again Enid had the impression of escaping, the warm lull of an engine driving her away. She wanted to go on as she was, forever driving, following the daylight over the rim of the world. But Dafydd Jones was not fast enough. The night was behind her, waiting to catch her and take her back.

"Did you know they have surrounded the mountains?" Dafydd Jones asked.

"No."

"Police," he said. "Checking every vehicle leaving."

"I didn't know."

"There is no way out, see?"

"I am glad you told me."

"It is not much I can do to help, but if there is anything . . ."

"Thank you," Enid murmured.

Caeravon was built around a central green with chestnut trees and a church. A twilight place amid the dark and light. Dafydd Jones stopped the car outside a tall Regency house. Silhouettes of people moved in the lighted rooms behind drawn blinds.

"Wait, shall I?"

"No," said Enid. "He will come."

"Aye," said Dafydd Jones. "He will come if it is necessary. Good enough in that way is Price-Jones."

Enid bit her lips. She had this one last chance to change her mind.

"It is necessary," she said softly. "There is no other way."

14

People did not work on the bank holiday, did not turn out on a cold Easter Sunday evening. Dr. Price-Jones was not being gracious. Surgery was on Tuesday, he told her.

Enid did not lose her temper. The shaking was inside her but her voice was calm enough. She was not suffering from the neurosis after a broken marriage, she was not being hysterical. He must come because he was needed, she would not ask otherwise. His questions were curt to the point of rudeness but he could not refuse to visit a sick old man. With the sound of *Messiah* playing on his stereo equipment. Dr. Price-Jones went to fetch his bag.

He did not speak to her on the journey back to Llanysted and she did not speak to him until they were into the village and he was not sure of the way. In the almost-dark the lights were bright in the chapel windows and the police car was pale parked at the end of the lane. They were not stopped, but they were noted.

The doctor glanced at Enid. "Don't give up, do they?" he said quietly.

"No," said Enid grimly.

"Must have been quite near your place."

"Just on the other side of the mountain."

"Any idea what it was?"

"None."

"Funny affair."

"Yes," said Enid. "Very funny."

He stopped the car, waited for her to get out and open the gate, then pulled into the yard. He had not been to High Valley Farm since Mrs. Thomas died, but the place had not changed. In the headlights he could see the ramshackle out-buildings, the dingy-whitewashed walls of the farmhouse. No place for a woman, this. No place for a sick old man either. Dr. Price-Jones sighed and reached for his bag. He knew what he was in for. Hywel Thomas had no use for doctors.

Enid walked up the long yard. Bright and high shone the frosty stars and the Mawrrhyn crouched black against the last paleness of the sky. The house in its darkness seemed to wait, a stone place, brooding and intimidating. She could not challenge the forces of stars and stone, but she was not afraid to face her own family when she knew she was right.

The car door slammed and the doctor was with her.

"Be a sharp one tonight."

"Frost," said Enid.

"Like living here, do you? After Cardiff?"

"It is better than nowhere."

"It *is* nowhere. Wherever you go around here you get the same feeling . . . mountains and sky and people scratching a living . . . as if it all belongs to something wilder . . . some kind of power that refuses to die. Can't see why people stay, myself."

"What makes you stay?" Enid asked.

"Good point," said Dr. Price-Jones. "Because I'm Welsh, I suppose, as if that explains everything."

He ducked under the low porch roof and she led him through a hallway that was dark and damp and smelling of dog, into a room full of light and the silence of people who were not pleased to see him. A black-and-white sheep dog growled and slunk under the table. No one spoke.

"Come in, please," Enid said.

He stood, tall and gray-haired, a stranger taking in the scene. And they were hostile and unwelcoming. Slowly the old man leaned forward, knocked out his pipe on the fire gate, looked at Enid.

"It is done then, girlie?"

Her head lifted slightly. "Yes, it is done."

"Mom!" said Gwyneth. "How could you!"

Rhys said nothing but his eyes slaughtered her. She did not care. There would be time enough later for words and recriminations.

"What is this?" Dr. Price-Jones said angrily.

He did not really need to ask. He was not here for an old man with a cough. He was here for the boy on the sofa with his face white as death and his hair so fair it was almost colorless. He knew who he was, of course. He was the one from the crashed plane. The one half the police force of Gwent were out looking for. The one a couple of hundred armed troops were scouring the mountains to find. Very young he was to be driving a plane. Strange, beautiful, hurt. The doctor felt pity move with his anger.

"You will see to him, please," Enid said.

But it was not that simple.

He looked at her, at Rhys and Gwyneth and the old man watching.

"You realize I should report this?"

"But you will not," Enid said definitely. "You are under the hypocritical oath."

"Hippocratic, Mom," Gwyneth murmured.

"Oath or not, I am bound to report it."

"Aye, well," said Hywel Thomas dryly. "Get on and report it then."

"I'll take a look at him first."

"You will not!"

Dr. Price-Jones raised an eyebrow. He had met Hywel Thomas before, and others like him, old men with faded eyes and weather-brown faces. Difficult, stubborn old men with their rough justice and their unbending pride. Nothing for nothing he would get from Hywel Thomas. And the dog growled at him from under the table, showed her fangs. Her eyes were gold in the light, fierce and unfriendly, like the eyes of the people. Threatening him.

"You let him be!" Hywel Thomas said. "He is asking nothing of you! Never asked you to come here. Be off on your tittle-tattling!"

"Father!" Enid said warningly.

The doctor stayed calm. "Manage without me, can you, Mr. Thomas?"

"No, he cannot," Enid said quickly.

"Managed before with no help from you," the old man growled.

"Aye," said Dr. Price-Jones as he turned and put down his bag. "And one of these days you will manage once to often. How long has he been like this?"

"There," Enid said thankfully. "You can sit down, Father. The doctor will see to him now. He has come for the job, see? Nothing more."

Nothing more.

But they did not believe her in the silence, Rhys and Gwyneth with their tight lips and hostile eyes. And the old man was mutinous and muttering. They were blaming her for the betrayal. But she could not help the hate and the unforgiveness. It was too late now to go back. She had brought the doctor here for Erlich, and someone had to answer him.

"How long?"

"Twenty-four hours."

"Like this? In the coma?"

Enid hesitated.

"He has been like it since this morning," Gwyneth said primly. "He was conscious for a while."

"Say anything, did he? Who he is? Where he came from?"

"No," said Gwyneth.

"I don't believe you, of course,"

"That's your privilege," said Rhys.

It was a privilege to be dragged out to this godfor-saken place, to tend an injured boy who was wanted by the authorities. A privilege to be tricked here by lies and met with abuse and a wall of conspiracy. Dr. Price-Jones didn't see how privilege came into it. Yet he was indeed privileged. He was here in the room with this boy. Allowed to touch him and discover. His hands, gentle and knowing, probed and pressed.

"What's under the bandage?"

"A bullet wound."

"They shot him then?"

"Yes."

"Typical. Shoot first and ask questions later. Old Parry told me there was shooting. How much blood has he lost?"

"A fair amount," said Rhys.

"Gallons," said Gwyneth.

"Mmm," muttered Dr. Price-Jones. "Could be

that's what's causing the unconsciousness. Or it could be this bruise on his head. There's no sign of a skull fracture but I can't be sure without an X ray. I've never seen anything quite like it, to be honest. Like some kind of cataleptic state . . . suspended animation . . . he's slowed down his body functioning to just a shade above death. Look at this . . . heartbeat, pulse . . . almost imperceptible . . . never seen anything like it."

"You can do something, though, can't you?" Gwyneth said anxiously.

The doctor sat back on his heels, ran a hand through his hair.

"I don't know."

"You're bound to know," Rhys said impatiently.

"Am I?"

The man rose, stood looking down on Erlich, trying to, believe the unbelievable.

"I know one thing," said Dr. Price-Jones. "That all I have known amounts to nothing, and all I do know is reduced to ignorance. This boy is not human!"

The room was quiet except for the slip of coals on the fire and the thump of Blod's tail on the linoleum. A vastness and stillness was all around them, the soul of the Mawrrhyn seeping through the roof and walls. In the deep silence, Erlich belonged to her, to a world of shadows and folklore that was not theirs. And they were standing there, helpless in their own world, and they did not know what to do.

"What d'you mean . . . not human?" Enid asked at last.

"What he says," said Rhys. "Not human."

"Different from us, is he?"

"That's right. Different."

"Not human," muttered Dr. Price-Jones. "Not of this earth."

"So there we are, then," Hywel Thomas said.

"You knew, did you, Mr. Thomas?"

"Knew the minute I clapped eyes on him. Not of us, I said."

"Where's he come from then?"

"Her," said Hywel Thomas.

"Who?"

"Mawrrhyn. He is hers."

"Rubbish, man!"

"He has the fairness, see?"

"You are saying he is out of the mountain? Like the fairy stories? Rubbish! Legend, that is. He's no legend. He's real. So where's he come from? Down from the sky? Out of that thing? And what was that thing?"

"Glyn Morris said it was a flying saucer," Enid murmured.

The doctor pounded his palm with his fist. "I can't believe that!"

"Not of this earth, you said."

"But I can't believe . . ."

"Maybe we are not meant to believe," Enid said softly.

"Hers," said Hywel Thomas. "She had claimed him, the Mawrrhyn. It is not for us to wonder on the likes of him."

Frost in the air made the fire burn brighter. Heat scorched the back of Gwyneth's legs, but Erlich was cold, his skin cold to the touch, dry cold. She wanted to warm him with the fingers of flame. She wanted to draw him closer, cover him with herself. His breathing was so shallow she couldn't be sure he breathed at all and his pulse threaded slower than the clock ticked, so that he seemed to die between the spaces of the seconds. And they with their shocked words talked on.

"Does it matter?" Gwyneth screamed. "Does it

matter who or what he is? He's hurt! That's human
enough. He needs help. That's human too. We've got
to help him!"

"There's not much I *can* do," said Dr. Price-Jones.

"But you can do something! You've got to!"

"And risk killing him? I daren't give him blood or
antibiotics. I don't know what's broken, if anything. He
might simply be suffering from exposure, or his blood
level might be critically low. I can't tell! I need tests,
X rays, laboratory facilities. This boy has got to get to
the hospital, and fast."

"No!" shrieked Gwyneth. "No! You can't do that!"

"You must see him here," Enid said.

"Do you really expect me to take that responsibility?" Dr. Price-Jone asked.

There was a short, sharp pause.

Then they gave up. Gwyneth was on her knees, her
head resting against Erlich, crying quietly. And under
the table the dog cried, sound in her throat, begging.
Enid turned bitterly away, and the old man nodded.
He had expected nothing of a doctor anyway. Only
Rhys stayed, young eyes locked and holding him,
stubborn.

"You're not taking him to the hospital," Rhys said.

Only for a few seconds more the doctor stood unmoving.

"You're not taking him. I'll kill him first."

Dr. Price-Jones nodded, took off his jacket, and
rolled up his shirt sleeves.

"Let's get these bandages off then, shall we?"

15

The car pulled away down the lane, the funnels of its headlights thrusting against the dark. Rhys watched it down the long mile to Llanysted, watched until the silence grew loud around him, then dragged shut the gate and drove the bolt home. Hoarfrost came off on his hands. "Brr." He thrust them under his armpits and turned to go in. "That's it then." It was too late to change the course of things. He could only trust that Dr. Price-Jones would keep his mouth shut. "And if he doesn't," said Rhys, "what's he get out of it?"

Beyond and behind the house the mountains were whitened with moonlight, scarred with black shadows. Grotesque and eerie the Mawrrhyn stood against the skyline, below the stars. Suddenly he wanted to go, up there to the high places, but instead he stared upward, and upward again to the sky. Stars where Erlich had come from. "Which one?" Rhys asked. They were fierce and brilliant, near and terribly far. The distance appalled him, and the power.

"Brr. Don't stand out here speculating!"

In the kitchen Enid was ironing. The air was fragrant with the scent of warm sheets, clean with clothes airing over the stove. Erlich's torn white shirt hung smooth over the back of a chair, ready for mending. Rhys fingered it. Finely woven, exquisitely sewn.

"Made in Hong Kong," Rhys said. "Would you believe it?"

Enid didn't answer him. The ironing board creaked.

"Do you have to do that at this time of night?" Rhys asked.

"Someone has to."

"It's bank holiday Sunday."

"What about it?"

"Why don't you knock off and enjoy yourself?"

"Mind out of the way," Enid said.

She was curt with him, her face harsh in the harsh light, annoyed about something. Her lips were set tight and her expression sour. You did not argue with Enid in that kind of mood. Rhys moved, watched her as she spread and folded Gwyneth's blouse. The movements of her hands were quick and competent, hands that had clipped and caressed him over the years. Enid coped in her own way no matter what happened. She had coped this time with no thanks from anyone, but Rhys hadn't seen it like that.

"It's all over now, Mom," Rhys said.

"Yes," said Enid. "It is over."

"Let's forget it then, shall we?"

"I didn't bring you up to be rude," Enid said.

"Who was rude?"

"You were. To the doctor."

"Well, I'm sorry about that."

"Rude, you were. Making threats."

"I said I'm sorry."

"I brought him here because it was necessary."

"Yes, I realize that now."

"And I was treated like a criminal in my own home!"

"Oh, come on, Mom. That's laying it on a bit."

"Is it? You and Gwyneth! You forget I'm your mother!"

"I wasn't thinking of you," Rhys said.

Enid looked at him. Then she did not look at him. She knew whom he had been thinking of. So had she. She took the shirt from the chair, held it to her, like it was a child, precious. They were all of them criminal. Traitors they were. Betraying their country, even the world, in helping Erlich. It was like he was more important than love or family or Captain Willoughby-Smythe. Slowly Enid stroked the shirt and her eyes took on a strange, vacant look. She was staring at the wall but she was not seeing. It was if she saw through it, out beyond.

"What will happen to him?" she asked.

"I don't know," said Rhys.

"He can't stay here, can he?"

"No."

"Then he'll have to go, won't he?"

"I guess so."

"How?" Enid asked. "And where?"

"I don't know," Rhys said again.

He hadn't thought about it, hadn't thought about anything. But he knew it wasn't long. Not long before the police or the soldiers traced Erlich here. He chewed his lip. Cardiff was the nearest place. He could take Erlich there, find some shabby lodging where they would be lost among a few million anonymous people. But they would need money to stay in Cardiff and

Enid had none to spare. Rhys would have to contact his father or maybe take a job to keep them.

The bar of the stove turned and squeaked under his hands. Cardiff provided no long-term answer. There was nowhere on this earth that Erlich could go to escape, and Rhys didn't know how to get from here to a star.

"There is no way out," Enid murmured. "Not into our world. Only back into her world, and for that we must pay."

Rhys frowned, glanced at her. "Pay who?"

"The Mawrrhyn."

She stroked the shirt and talked, not to him but to herself.

"It is no good, see? No good going into our world for help because we don't know enough. But she knows. She has the power, same as he does. She has been there since the beginning. She knows how to cross time, but we die. You ask her."

Rhys stared. "Are you telling me that mountain has intelligence?"

"When I was a girl I used to feel her."

"The Mawrrhyn?"

"That's right. Very strong she was, her presence outside, like a living person. Woman, she is, in her mind and her soul. Part of me knew her."

"You're joking, of course."

"Of course," Enid murmured. "I am joking. People cannot live with that kind of knowing. That's why I left, see? I was only fifteen. Went to Cardiff, I did, and she didn't matter there. That kind of thing is dead under dust and concrete and traffic fumes. In the cities people do not heed. All those years I was forgetting her. Then he came."

"Who?"

"Erlich. The old man knew, and I was not admitting

it. He knows Erlich is like her, but I must make him ordinary because I cannot be fifteen again. Only when I look at him there is a chord that strikes and I do not know what to do about the feelings inside me. It is too much to admit, see? Too much to think about. If I try thinking about it, it will swamp me. I cannot cope with those kinds of powers, the power in Erlich and the power of the mountain."

Rhys could not believe what he saw, what he heard.

Enid was not acting like his mother. She was some strange mystical woman, a woman with a Welsh voice lilting, talking of some deep, inaccessible power that lay in earth and in people. Enid had never given any account to those kinds of things. Now suddenly it was all coming out, like the old man telling stories of Morgan and Gwydion and the lady of the Mawrrhyn, as if down underneath she always had believed.

"You don't really believe it, do you," Rhys asked.

She stroked, not hearing him.

"It is born in us," Enid said. "But most of us go through life without ever knowing. Then something happens to wake us, and it comes on so strong that you feel you could break through. But you never do. The feeling slips, and there you are, back again, trapped in this world. And Erlich is trapped with us because we don't know how to help him. Only she knows, she waits, and we cannot pay her."

Rhys shook his head.

He was lost. He could feel but not recognize the sense of what she was saying. It was too deep, too obscure. He was locked out by his own logic. It was like listening to a legend. Plausible enough until you stopped to think. But Enid wasn't thinking. She was miles away. The words didn't mean anything. Or maybe they did. Maybe she had some idea at the back of her mind, something positive behind the blank of her eyes.

"Mom?"

"We cannot pay her. She is asking too much of us."

"Mom?"

"Too much of life and regret."

She stroked, deaf, and blind.

"Oy! Mom!"

Enid jumped. Suddenly she was aware of room space and time. She glanced at Rhys. Guilty. He had caught her daydreaming and she had supper to think about. She dropped the shirt over the back of the chair and rummaged in the washing basket. The old man's long johns were damp around the legs. Steam rose from the hot iron, and in the other room Gwyneth was laughing. Enid had that much to be thankful for. It had not all been wasted, bringing Dr. Price-Jones here. Erlich was better now, awake and fed.

"What did you say?" she asked Rhys.

"It's what you said."

"What was that?"

"Nonsense, most of it."

"Oh well, we can't be perfect all of the time."

"You said that the mountain was real."

"And what's wrong with that? She is real, right enough. You look at her. She's outside right now. Mawrrhyn. There is no escaping from her living here."

"You didn't mean it like that," Rhys said. "Ask her, you said."

Enid rested the flats of her hands on the ironing board. For a moment she did not speak.

"What will you do, then?" she said.

"You mean . . . will I ask her? A lump of granite?"

"I mean about Erlich."

Rhys shrugged. "Cardiff, I suppose."

"And how are you going to get to Cardiff?"

"Walk? Hitch? Ride a bike?"

"With him?"

"He's got legs."

"You've not heard, then? They're guarding the roads."

Rhys sat quietly in the old man's chair. The starched tablecloth rustled like paper. Ashes lay dead in the hearth, blew in a draft. He could hear mice scratching behind the baseboard, and in the front room Gwyneth laughed. There was nothing to laugh about. There was no way out of here. No way. Only up, over the Mawrrhyn, into her world.

Rhys glanced at his mother. She must have known. Across the mountains it was less than eight miles to Cwmvanwy, and from there it was only a short trip down the valley to pick up the main Swansea-Cardiff road. They wouldn't be guarding that route. They wouldn't think anyone would be mad enough to try it at night. But it was full moon and Rhys knew the mountains.

"We can go over the mountains," Rhys said.

Enid stood very still. "In broad daylight? With the soldiers out searching?"

"We can go at night," Rhys said.

Enid said nothing. Her hand on the iron did not move it. The smell of burning grew strong. She stood until the smoke began to curl, then she unplugged the iron and put it away, folded the burned cloth and the ironing board, and opened a can of baked beans for supper. When she finally looked at Rhys her expression was bitter.

"When are you planning on going, then?" Enid asked.

16

"I think you're out of your mind!" Gwyneth said to Rhys.

"Except that he is not," Erlich said softly.

"You can't cross those mountains at night!"

"Yes we can," Rhys said obstinately.

"I already have," Erlich reminded her.

"Yes," Gwyneth said grimly. "And just look at yourself."

Erlich looked down.

Tights and tunic shirt. He was as he should be, as he used to be. On the surface physically perfect. The bandages tight around his ribs didn't show. The cut on his head was healing.

"There's nothing much wrong with me that I can see."

"Don't pretend!"

"I'm not. I'm almost like new."

"You can't even stand without holding on to that chair!"

Erlich let go and the pain bit him. His jaw set stiff as he bore it.

"You see? I am perfectly capable."

But Gwyneth was no fool.

"You can't go over those mountains!"

"Can you think of another way?" Rhys asked.

Erlich had to go. It was not safe for him to stay here. The soldiers were too close. Hunted and hunting, he had to escape. He had said there were others like himself scattered throughout the cities of the earth. Maybe even now they were looking for him. But they wouldn't come here, not yet. Wouldn't walk into the traps set for one who might already be dead. They had no sure way of knowing Erlich was alive, but they would wait for him out beyond the edges of the search, wait for him among the crowds who did not notice the face of a stranger, in Cardiff or Newport or Swansea.

The plan Rhys had outlined made sense. But it was so fast and so final. It meant Erlich would leave before he had even stayed.

"You can't go today anyway," Gwyneth said definitely.

"I think I have to," Erlich said.

"You can wait for tomorrow and see how you are then."

"By tomorrow my luck may have run out."

"Go over the Mawrrhyn in the dark and it'll run out for sure!"

Erlich half smiled. "I have crossed many millions of dark miles."

"Cross that one and I'm telling you . . . you'll never make it!"

"Just a few short steps."

"You want to end up with a broken neck?"

"Don't dramatize," Rhys said. "It's not the Alps."

"I'm not dramatizing! I'm telling you."

"Just listen a minute, Gwyneth. . . ."

"No! You listen! Dr. Price-Jones said . . ."

"Dr. Price-Jones has no say in it."

"You won't get past Mom. . . ."

"I already have. She said nothing, so it's all settled."

"If it's all settled," Gwyneth said angrily, "why ask me?"

"Because you had to know, didn't you?" Rhys said.

"Thanks for nothing," Gwyneth said sourly.

She turned away, flung herself down in the armchair.

She was bitter and hating. She hated Rhys. Hated him because he was taking Erlich away. She had never hated anyone before. Never had a reason. She had felt it when they lived in Cardiff, but that was for her father and it wasn't her hate. Now it wrecked her, smashed through the warmth of her grandfather's house like a cold, destructive fist. Yesterday it had been the same between Rhys and Enid. Now it was Gwyneth's turn.

She stared at the fireplace, a landscape that was red and burning out of fire and coal, and she wished Rhys was in it, being destroyed. That suddenly he was out of existence, with no hurt and no leaving. That he did not stand real, behind her, insisting on something she didn't want to know. Erlich must go. She could actually feel Rhys forcing it on her in the silence, feel his hands move, the grip and squeak on the leather upholstery. He was waiting for her acquiescence.

"Why don't you go and stand by someone else?"

"Why should I?" Rhys said.

"You stink!"

"Do you have to make this personal?"

"You make me feel positively sick."

"Listen, thickhead! Just face facts, will you!"

"Sheep, that's what it is. Sheep stink!"

"What do you want for him then?" Rhys asked. "The Ministry of Defense jail?"

Gwyneth turned her back on him. She didn't want to speak.

She burned him slowly in the fire but he was still there behind her. There was a piece of cotton hanging loose from the hem of her skirt. She pulled and it unraveled. She wound and unwound it and wound it again, around and around the fingers of her hand. Tight, stopping the blood flow, making the ends whiten. Loose, watching the color flood. Concentrating. Strangling. Hair fell like blinders around her face, cut off the sight of the room. The day outside was harsh and colorless. She wanted nothing to do with any of it. It was senseless, and Gwyneth was used to sulking.

Rhys looked to Erlich, spread his hands. "Sorry. She gets like this sometimes."

"Why?" Erlich asked. "What have we done?"

"You're leaving, aren't you?"

"But I *can't* stay. You know I can't."

"*I* know," said Rhys. "But try telling her that."

Erlich moved, going over to Gwyneth. Winced, clutched the table for support.

"I'll give you a hand," Rhys offered.

"No," said Erlich. "I need some practice. I can make it."

He could make it in slow steps, gritting his teeth against the pain.

Blod woke suddenly from her sleep, watched him, and knew. It wasn't help Blod offered him, it was empathy. In the deep brown of her eyes Rhys saw Erlich's pain. Watched as Blod bore it until he was in the chair opposite Gwyneth, half dead from the effort.

Then she was with him, her body pressed against his legs, gazing up at him, mute and sharing. His head rested on her head. His breath dragged.

"Oh, Blod . . . tell me . . . it doesn't hurt . . . doesn't hurt." Sweat beaded his skin, darkened the pale of his hair. And his hands were in Blod's fur, gripping, wanting relief. "You know . . . you always know . . . tell me . . . it doesn't hurt." She licked his hands. "Tell me. . . . That's right." Licked as he fondled. Whined for him. "Blod."

It was senseless. Erlich wasn't fit enough to cross a room, let alone a mountain.

"So now you know," Gwyneth told Rhys crossly.

Rhys turned to stare out the window. They had the dogs out after Erlich.

"Have to think of something else, won't you?" Gwyneth said.

"Maybe we could wait a couple of days," Rhys said hopefully.

"Wait for what?" Erlich asked quietly.

"You," said Gwyneth. "You're not crossing the Mawrrhyn like that!"

Erlich coughed, clutched his ribs. "I'm all right, I tell you. I'm trained to endure a few bruises. It hurts, but that's all."

"And I hurt," Gwyneth said. "I'll fetch your tablets."

He was quiet when the tablets took effect, leaning back in the chair with his eyes closed. His hand dangled limp over the side, touched Blod like a benediction. And between him and Rhys, Gwyneth stood, Florence Nightingale in Welsh, with her hands on her hips.

"Well?" she demanded of Rhys. "What are you waiting for?"

Rhys raised an eyebrow. "Him. Who else? We haven't finished discussing . . ."

"He will not be discussing anything," Gwyneth said.

"Oh, come off it. . . ."

"He's resting."

"Jump down, will you!"

"And you get out!"

"What?"

"Go on . . . get out. Go and jump in the lake. Boil your head. Count sheep. Anything. But leave him alone!"

"I see," Rhys said stiffly. "Count sheep, is it?"

"Yes, and count the odds while you're at it."

"Want him all to yourself, do you?"

"You've done enough damage for one morning!" Gwyneth howled.

"Very well," Rhys said. "I'll go then. I can take a hint."

"Take Blod!" Gwyneth said. "Never mind the hint."

Rhys stared at her from the doorway.

She was nuts. She could no more give Blod away than she could make Erlich stay. Blod had no intention of going with Rhys. Her tailed wagged him a slight acknowledgment, but she wouldn't go with him. She was Erlich's now, belonging to him heart and soul. Blod the dog, the two-faced bitch. Rhys had no power over that kind of loving. And Gwyneth had no power over it either. Erlich belonged to the stars.

"You're a fool," said Rhys. "Over the hill! You want to try thinking?"

Then he was gone.

Gwyneth bit her lip, bent to sweep up the loose ashes on the hearth. Wind whined down the chimney and the house seemed suddenly empty. She could hear dog voices baying cold out on the hills. Cold where Rhys had gone, leaving her vulnerable, leaving

her alone with Erlich. Blod whined slightly in answer
to those other dogs. Gwyneth was a fool. Even now
they were tracking Erlich down, his trail in the icy water, frozen in moss and bog, lost under frost that was
thick as snow. They wouldn't give up until they found
him, and nothing Gwyneth could do would alter that.

"I have to go, Gwyneth," Erlich said softly.

There was gray dust between the tiles.

"I can't stay to be caught. They want more than I
can give. You know that, don't you? I can't stay. Even
one more day could be too long."

Ashes to ashes, dust to dust.

Gwyneth knew, but she had to make one last try.
"So you'll die, will you? Out there on the mountains?"

"If I have to," Erlich said quietly.

Gwyneth hung up the brush and shovel, sat back
on her heels.

She had always known. Known the moment he
came that he would have to go. He was just a jewel
flash in her lifetime. You couldn't hold on to that kind
of magic. Like a fairy tale, he had stepped down out
of stars. He was beautiful and happening until the
words ran out of time. When the darkness came he
would walk out of here, out into the killing wind, out
of her life. He would go with Rhys over the mountains
and she would never see him again.

She turned to face him.

Like summer he was, with his fair gold hair and his
blue eyes.

"No more to say then, is there?" Gwyneth said.

17

"She's nuts," said Rhys.

"Who's nuts?" said Enid.

"Our Gwyneth. She's stuck on him."

"Not that way, is she?"

"I reckon. You should have heard her."

"I heard only the row."

"*You* never said anything."

"I am not stuck on him that way."

"But you never said *anything.*"

"Would it have made any difference?"

"Probably not."

"Well then."

They walked up the lane together, Rhys and Enid. The land was around them, hard as iron, without softness or color. There was no shelter in that exposed place. The wind crept cold down from the mountains, blew bitter in their faces. They could hear dog voices trailing far and clear over the moors, and lower down the valley a tractor churred slowly over the bitten fields by Hughes Farm. The afternoon seemed timeless.

They were caught in a limbo, between what had happened and what would happen, between the world of the valley and the world of the mountain, and they were belonging to neither time or place. Only the sky made a link between them. Only the same cold bit through them.

Rhys turned up his collar.

The sky was an overall gray, seeming to lean heavy on the shoulder of the Brechin, hang low and sullen over the fir trees, arch gloom above the valley. It seemed threatening in some way, almost like snow. It had him trapped with the dogs and the sheep cries, the shouts of the searchers and the farmer calling his cattle. He could see his breath rising white. He could see the smoke from the cottages bend and drift.

"At least they are inside," Enid said.

Dafydd Jones' red sedan was parked on the wasteland opposite, and up behind the houses a police car was parked by the open gate of the plantation. Rhys stopped walking.

"That's it, then. The peat road's out."

"They might not be guarding the other end," Enid said.

"That would help, would it?"

"You could cut up through the woods from the bottom."

"Along the square on the hypotenuse," Rhys muttered.

"Worth looking at, isn't it?"

"Maybe," said Rhys.

"Easier than going up the Mawrrhyn if they're not guarding."

"Yes. If."

"Well, you can go and see, can't you?"

Enid was going to borrow a thermos and knapsack from Dafydd Jones.

Rhys left her, cut across the common to the wood. It was thawing fast. Wheels had churned the track into mud. It clogged his boots, dragged at his feet. Gorse clawed the legs of his trousers. There was a wall around the wood, green with winter lichen, and topped with barbed wire to keep the sheep out. Rhys had no choice but to use the gateway.

He knew what would happen.

The policeman slammed the car door.

"Where are you going, boyo?"

"In there," Rhys said calmly. "Where else?"

"Public's not allowed in there."

"It's National Trust, isn't it?"

"Not allowed. Sorry."

"So who left the gate open then?" Rhys demanded.

The policeman looked surprised.

"Wide open," Rhys said. "And at the other end. Them sheep'll strip the young trees if I don't fetch them out. I don't see why the old man should pay fines to the forestry for other people's carelessness."

"You got sheep in there?"

"That's right. Half a dozen down at the far end."

"Better fetch them out then, hadn't you?"

"That's why I came," said Rhys.

"Manage on your own, can you?"

"The dog's in heat."

"Well, rather you than me," the policeman said.

Rhys entered the wood, trees growing quietly together where the wind did not penetrate. It was almost warm. But still there was that gray stony silence, a stillness wherein nothing moved but himself. He kept to the side of the track, picked his way through the sodden grass and dead undergrowth. The ground oozed with melting frost. The murk of the sky seemed to press down on him. The leaves dripped.

"So much for moonlight," Rhys muttered.

It was depressing.

Where the woods gave way to the open moors Rhys saw the mobile army headquarters, a parked van with a radio aerial. And all round it were jeeps and tents and trucks, cooking quarters, and a canvas latrine. Camped, they were, right at the edge of the peat road. Rhys leaned on the gate. He'd been right about that . . . it *was* open, but everything else was useless. He watched for a while the comings and goings, the string of soldiers searching out on the stretched skyline, then turned his face the other way.

Beyond the ridge of the Brechin the valley fell away. And beyond the valley the Mawrrhyn rose, gray and stark, her cragged summit lost in the cloud. "There is no way out," Enid had said. "Only up into her world, and for that we must pay." And up into her world Rhys and Erlich would have to go.

"But I'll not pay you," Rhys said.

If the Mawrrhyn acknowledged, it was with silence. She was dangerously still. Yet somehow he felt she was alive and knowing he was there. It was a sinister feeling. Her breath touched him in the wind, cruel and icy, and his lips split with the cold. He shivered, licked the sore salt taste of blood, thrust his hands deep into his pockets. He wanted to return menace for menace.

"We'll beat you, lady," Rhys said. "You'll see."

His words were lost in the sound of an engine, the bang and jolt of a Land-Rover as it came toward him. He glanced around at it. Willoughby-Smythe! That was all he ever did . . . rode around in a Land-Rover looking smart. Rhys waited for the inevitable polite small talk. The Land-Rover slowed and stopped.

"Hello, Rhys."

"Good afternoon, sir."

"What brings you out here?"

"I'm reporting for the *Brynllan Observer*. What brings you?"

The army captain smiled. "I'm surprised the police didn't stop you."

"They did, actually."

"But they let you through. What for?"

"Sheep," said Rhys.

"Ah," said Captain Willoughby-Smythe. "Sheep."

"In the plantation," said Rhys. "Doing damage to the trees."

"You've come to round them up, then?"

"That's right."

"No dog?"

"Blod's in heat."

"And your grandfather?"

"He's putting his feet up."

"I thought maybe he was ill."

"Who? Grandad? He's fitter than you are. Race you up them mountains any day. And me probably."

Captain Willoughby-Smythe nodded, watched Rhys thoughtfully.

"I'm glad about that," he said at last. "Because I noticed the doctor called at your place this morning. He was there last night too. I thought maybe the old man was ill."

It was a trap and Rhys had fallen for it.

"Yes, well . . . he goes up and down, you know. Last night he wasn't feeling too good, so Mom called Dr. Price-Jones, to be on the safe side. It's the cough, see. Gets down on his chest this time of year. Never can tell at his age and Mom wanted to be sure. He just needs rest and medicine, that's why I'm . . . Excuse me now. I got to go and see to them sheep."

He went unhurriedly down the steep slope, following the wall through trees and brambles and dead bracken. There was a fear inside him. He wanted to run but didn't dare. He knew Willoughby-Smythe was still there, watching him. That man was smart in more ways than one. Keen in his mind he was, trained to observe. He didn't miss a move, not the twitch of a muscle, not the flicker of an eyelid. Smiled, he did. Flashed his white teeth. And all the time behind his smile, behind his eyes, was something cool and calculating, waiting to pounce. He knew Rhys had lied.

The man watched him until he was out of sight, then drove on down the track. He was not smiling now.

And he was not smiling when Enid met him coming out of Dafydd Jones' house with the thermos and knapsack. He was polite to her. He offered her a lift. But she felt something was missing, that perhaps for some reason he was not quite liking her. He didn't seem warm or glad to see her. His face was expressionless and he didn't speak as he drove her down to the farm.

The Land-Rover slowed outside the gate and he turned off the engine. She thought he would stop and talk, but he leaned across her and opened the door. Very near to her he was, for just a moment, but he sat back and the moment was gone.

"You will not come in for tea, then?"

"Later, perhaps," he said briefly.

"Away to Brynllan, are you?"

"Duty calls."

"I will not hold you up then," Enid said primly.

The disappointment lodged in the pit of her stomach. She was to go and he would not stop her. He had not been like this before, remote and unconcerned, leaving her to cope in a bleak empty place without sympathy. His distance hurt. And she was angry with herself for being a fool. She dragged at her coat caught between the seat gap. Hands that were not hers pulled it free.

She looked at him.

"Why didn't you tell me?" he asked her.

"Tell you what?"

"That you were needing a doctor for your father."

"I didn't know at the time."

"Chapel," he said. "And I would have driven you to Caeravon."

"Yes, well . . . there it is. I was not thinking straight."

"No," he said softly. "You were not thinking straight. Nor was I. Nor was someone else I could mention. People seldom do think straight in a crisis."

He was staring ahead of him, his eyes on the landscape, his fingers drumming on the steering wheel. The air through the door was as bitter as his voice, and Enid began to sweat.

"What do you mean?" Enid asked.

"Nothing," he said heavily.

"You know something I don't."

"I know nothing . . . except what I hear and what I read. Dr. Price-Jones to High Valley Farm . . . once last night and once this morning . . . for a sick old man with bronchial pneumonia . . . according to our traffic census. But you never told me. Is he going to the hospital?"

"This is his home," Enid said curtly.

"And you can manage everything without my help?"

"I can cope, thank you."

He nodded, and again she noted the bitter twist of his lips.

"I am bound to admire the way you are coping," he said grimly.

But it was not admiration in his voice. It was something cold and sad. Enid stood in the road clutching the knapsack, and he started the engine.

"I may see you later," he said.

And it was not a promise he left her with.

It was a threat.

18

Enid was cooking Welsh cakes over the stove. From the old man's chair Erlich watched her, and in the chair by the table Hywel Thomas sat puffing on his pipe. The kitchen filled with a warm brown smell of cooking, filled with blue tobacco smoke that made curls around the light. Outside, the day grew later, gathered toward dark, and closed them in. Cozy.

"Ought to go on like this," Rhys said.

"What should?" Enid asked.

"Life," said Rhys. "Us, like we are now."

"It is home," said Hywel Thomas. "That is why."

But it wouldn't be home for much longer. They were going soon, Rhys and Erlich. With a newspaper between his feet, Rhys pried chunks of dried mud from Gwyneth's walking boots. He felt the time draining away. He felt his reluctance growing.

Enid flipped the cakes.

Two cans of tomato soup stood ready on the cabinet. Two pairs of woolen socks hung warming, and she had borrowed extra bread from Mrs. Owen-Morgan. It was all organized, everything ready. It just needed Rhys to decide.

"Well?" Enid demanded. "You going or aren't you?"

"I don't know," Rhys said.

"Better make up your mind, hadn't you?"

"There's plenty of time."

"And there's plenty to do. Sandwiches. Clothes."

"And how long will that take? Five minutes? We're not going for a fortnight's camping to the South Pole."

"You will need to wrap up warm, won't you?"

"Aye," said Hywel Thomas. "It is cold on the mountains at night."

Rhys didn't want to go, didn't want to leave the warm bright kitchen.

"I'd wait," he said thoughtfully. "If it wasn't for him."

"Who?" said Enid.

"Willoughby-what's-it."

Enid went still. "Saw him, did you? This afternoon? What did he say?"

"It's what he didn't say," said Rhys. "He's sly, that one."

"He's a decent, feeling human being," said Enid.

"He is English," said Hywel Thomas. "Paid by the government."

"Yes," said Rhys. "And I don't trust him."

Enid turned sharply away, put the cooked cakes to cool on a rack, and put a fresh batch on to cook on the hot surface of the stove. She was not easy in herself. All this waiting to go and not saying when was making her jumpy. She brushed back her hair with a floury hand.

"So you are going, then? Because of what the English army captain did not say?"

"I don't know," Rhys said again.

Enid turned to Erlich. "What about you? You ready to go, are you?"

"If I have to," Erlich said.

"That's the spirit, boyo," Hywel Thomas said. "Manage lovely, we will, you and me . . . the old and the wounded bringing up the rear."

"You coming with us then, Grandad?" Rhys asked.

"No," said Enid. "Most definitely he is not."

"Show them the way, see?"

"They can find their way without you."

"Me and Blod," the old man said obstinately. "Over Mawrrhyn and as far as the next valley."

Enid slammed down the cutter. Fluted shapes of dough littered the table.

"Now you listen to me!" Enid said. "I have enough worry without a damned fool old man taking it into his head to go walking the Mawrrhyn at night! Do you think I feel easy letting Rhys . . ."

"Don't!" Erlich said sharply.

He was bent forward, his face in the shadow, but they could see his strain. His fingers were knotted in Blod's fur and there was a stillness about him. He was staring fixedly at a patch of spilled flour on the grimy mat. Blod licked him and whined but she could not reach him. The room was quiet and waiting and full of their breathing.

"What's the matter, lovey?" Enid asked. "Hurt, do you?"

"Yes," Erlich said.

"Give you some tablets, shall I?"

He lifted his face. "It is not that kind of hurt," he told her.

He was pale and taut, almost grim. His gaze went

from one to another, leveling them. He was not a boy, young and powerless. He was a star lord and they were under him, trapped by the blue of his eyes.

"You won't do this," Erlich said.

"Won't do what?" Rhys asked slowly.

"Anything! I know what's in you! I'm not making you! You will not hang on me the loss of life or limb! The death of an old man on a dark mountain! I can go alone. I don't ask you to come with me!"

The quietness held. Intense it was, deep like the common blood in their veins. And Erlich was a stranger among them, seeing and knowing them, releasing them from their obligation. They owed him nothing. They could see him go and forget he had ever been.

"Don't be stupid!" Rhys said gruffly.

"It is not for you to say who comes and who goes," said Hywel Thomas.

Erlich looked at Enid, brilliant his eyes, blue and burning her.

"You do not have to pay this price for me!"

"No," said Enid. "We do not have to."

"Then why will you?"

Enid shook her head. "I don't know. It is this way because there can be no other way. We do what we feel we must without asking why. Some things do not bear questioning. But it will take more than you, or I, or Rhys, or that silly old man, to change what will be. And you are not going over those mountains on your own."

Gwyneth sat in the small, stinking room. A can of disinfectant rusted in the corner. Spiders scuttled over the lime-washed walls, made webs among the rafters. The door was eaten by woodworms, and one tiny window let in the last gray traces of daylight. Wind whined cold through the broken pane. She could hear the chickens roosting. She could hear the rush of the stream over its stones. She heard a sheep cry in the distance. Gone home, they had, the soldiers and dogs. Given up and gone home. It was all quiet out there on the mountains.

Gwyneth frowned. It was too silent. Too absolute, too profound, almost as if the silence was deliberate. And not five minutes ago she had heard their voices up beyond the valley. She went quickly into the dusk, stood on the flagged path between the cabbages. The wind rattled the branches of the rowan tree and Gwyneth listened and watched.

There was nothing to see. The land rose empty up over the Brechin and the valley was dreary under twilight, gray and impenetrable. She was about to go in when beyond the paddock, where the stream flowed into the sheep dip and became her grandfather's property, she saw someone move. A shadow shifted among shadows, a shade by the twisted hawthorn tree. A man climbed from the gully of the stream, followed by another man and a dog on a leash. Gwyneth watched as they climbed the crumbling wall and went toward the barn.

"Older than Rhys, are you?" Enid asked.

"I am older," Erlich confirmed.

"Eighteen, is it? Nineteen?"

"You've got a nose like Concorde, Mom," Rhys said.

"I was only asking."

"And maybe he doesn't want to tell you."

"You don't mind telling me, do you?"

"I can't." Erlich looked at the old man. "You tell her."

"Aye." The old man nodded, stuffed his pipe. "Old,

see? Old as the mountains. Old as she is old. Before you or I or men were born. Old since the start of time. He cannot say how old he is."

"Don't talk nonsense," Enid said. "You've no idea."

"Except that it's true," Erlich murmured.

Enid paused from scraping up the loose flour, stood with the knife in her hand.

"What are you telling me?"

Erlich spread his hands. "You think I'm young? I'm not. I'm ageless. For me there is no time, not as you know it. You stay still in it, wait as it passes you, wither and die. But I travel it. I can overtake millions of your years in a few seconds. Only here, in your world, am I trapped in time. But you don't understand that, do you?"

"No," Enid said shortly.

"It's something to do with Einstein," Rhys said. "Relativity. If you go faster than light, time travels backward. Something like that."

"He's immortal, then?"

"Old," said Hywel Thomas.

"Immortal?"

"No," said Erlich. "Not immortal."

"He can die, Mom," said Rhys. "Just like us. Quick, with a bullet through his brain. Slow from pollution. Or tonight, break his neck on the Mawrrhyn."

Enid scraped flour into the slop bucket.

"You've made up your mind, then?" she asked.

But Rhys had no answer and there was no time.

Blod barked, sudden and deafening, leaped from her place by Erlich, and growled at the door. Her teeth showed white and sharp. Her hackles were raised.

Rhys dropped the boots he'd been cleaning. "What's up?"

"Someone's out there," said Hywel Thomas.

It was Gwyneth who came through from the scullery to stand with her back against the door. Her eyes were dark in the bright light and she was breathing hard. The wind had brought color to her cheeks, disheveled her hair. And still Blod growled, menacing her.

"Sit down, you crazy bitch!" the old man said.

She took no notice. She growled and closed in on Gwyneth, slow and vicious.

"Come here, darn you!"

Her eyes were without pity.

"Blod," said Gwyneth. "It's only me, Blod."

She was going to attack, but Erlich whistled. His voice came softly through her madness. "Here, Blod. Come to me. Come on."

She turned and went to him, lay under the arch of his legs. But her eyes stayed on the door and the growling stayed soft as a muttering in her throat. She was telling them someone was outside. Telling them she wanted to kill. And only the quiet touch of Erlich's hand forbade her.

"That dog is nasty!" Enid said.

"Nay," said Hywel Thomas. "She is not."

"She would have bitten our Gwyneth."

"She was mistaking things, that is all."

"Yes, and if she makes the same mistake again . . ."

"It doesn't matter, Mom," Gwyneth said.

"We are not keeping dangerous animals!"

"There are things happening worse than Blod! Out there! Two armed men just gone into our barn."

"What?"

"Soldiers with rifles, Mom. Gone into our barn!"

Rhys grabbed the knapsack.

"Right, then, that settles it. We're not waiting for tomorrow or moonrise. We're going now, soon as it's dark!"

19

Rhys piled things in the knapsack, rope and ground-sheet, string, adhesive tape, flashlight and compass, matches and penknife, spare socks, and a slab of chocolate. He put a packet of chewing gum in his anorak pocket, and Enid made sandwiches. It was all there, everything they would need for suvival if the worst came to the worst. He added the thermos of hot soup and half a dozen Welsh cakes. There was nothing else, only the tattered survey map that lay spread on the table. Rhys frowned, studied it for the last time. Over by Cwmvanwy he didn't know the mountains too well.

"What's this coal mine?"

"The Slag Pit," said Enid. "It is closed now."

"But the road's still there, isn't it?"

"I've not been that way since . . ."

"Grandad!" called Rhys. "Is there still a road by the Slag Pit?"

The old man came in from the dark scullery.

"Still a road? Aye. Or there was two years ago."

Enid sniffed. "You are looking like a walking rummage sale, Father."

Hywel Thomas didn't care much for appearances. He wore what he always wore when it was cold outside, and he must go and see to the sheep. His thick overcoat was belted with string, and string bound the legs of his trousers tight around the tops of his boots to stop them from flapping in the wind. His gray knitted hood was moth-holed to match his mittens.

"It is warmth that counts."

"It's the smell."

"Sheep smell. Healthy, that is."

"Yes," agreed Enid. "Outside in the paddock."

"And it is outside I am going," Hywel Thomas said. "Now in a minute, when people make up their minds."

"Okay," said Rhys. "We'll head for the Slag Pit."

He turned to Erlich. "You ready?"

Erlich looked strange, dressed in Gwyneth's jeans and sweater and walking boots, and Enid's knitted hat. Confused he was, in all the muddle of their talk and activity. He had organized the starting of a thousand journeys between world and world. He had navigated the vast distances between the stars. But here he was lost among them and he did not know if he was ready or not ready. His bewilderment showed.

"Coat," said Rhys.

"This?" asked Erlich, fingering Gwyneth's old navy-blue duffel.

"That's right," said Rhys. "Put it on."

Erlich dragged arms through sleeves, fumbled with the strange buttons.

"Here," said Enid. "Let me."

He was not golden or lordly in his borrowed clothes. He was a boy like Rhys, about to face a mountain, and maybe not wanting to any more than she wanted him to go. There was a finality in the room around her, Rhys and the old man waiting, and Blod's eyes shining dark and eager in the light. Enid felt a prickle of tears behind her eyes. Time ran out on her in the doing up of six wooden toggles, but she would not cry. She tried to smile.

"There you are, then."

"Thank you," Erlich said gravely.

"Ready, is he?" Rhys asked.

"Except for the gloves," said Enid.

"Gwyneth!" shouted Rhys. "Hurry up with them gloves!"

Upstairs, something slammed and Gwyneth came down loudly. She carried a pair of fur-backed mittens, and a pendant on a chain, which she hung around Erlich's neck.

"It is for you," Gwyneth said.

He cupped it in his hand, a cheap gaudy thing, a silver-covered medallion belonging to Granny Thomas before she died and now belonging to Gwyneth.

"What is it?" Erlich asked.

"Saint Christopher," said Gwyneth.

"Your God?" said Erlich. "And you are giving him to me?"

"He watched over travelers in the old times," Enid said.

"Where's mine?" Rhys asked.

"You don't need luck," Gwyneth said.

"I have nothing to give you in return," Erlich said.

"It doesn't matter," Gwyneth said lightly.

"We are not expecting repayment," Enid said.

"Just say good-bye," Rhys told him. "And get it over with."

Over with . . . all the years that had been and the years that would come. Rhys couldn't say good-bye, there were no words. There were no words for all the millions of things he might never say. There was a lump in his throat as he stared at Gwyneth and his mother. He hadn't known it would be like this. It seemed like the end of everything, like the second before the curtain ¯came down on the last scene of the last performance and he would never act again, not here, not with them.

"Mom?" said Rhys.

"Don't," said Enid.

"There's nothing left, Mom!"

"There is this place. It will be here when you come back."

But she wouldn't be.

Rhys turned away. He couldn't stand the knowing. He stood with his back to all of them. And Blod whined, thrust her nose into his hand. Eyes that were dark with loving gazed up into his own. Blod knew what was ending. She had come back to him, the last comfort, the last caring. . . . He pulled her ear.

"Let's go," Rhys said.

His voice was a signal. There were no more excuses, no more delays, no more time . . . only the few seconds the old man took to fetch his walking stick, a few seconds for Rhys to bend and untwist the straps of the knapsack.

"Have you got everything?" Enid asked.

"There's the map," said Erlich.

"I can remember," said Rhys.

"Take it," said Enid. "Best to be on the safe side."

"And don't crumple it," said Gwyneth. "Fold it properly."

Rhys muttered, dropped the knapsack, folded the map slowly along its brittle lines. And in the dark behind the old man's legs, Blod growled. Her lips curled above the sound and her teeth showed white. In the stiff, sudden silence they were listening. They heard footsteps, someone walking briskly over the cobbles of the yard. Again Blod growled. A knock came on the door and she barked madly. Barked. And all they could do was stare at each other, frozen in stillness.

"What do we do?" Rhys asked wildly.

"I bet it's him," said Gwyneth. "Mom's fancy army man!"

"He has come for me," Erlich said quietly.

"If it's army," said Hywel Thomas darkly, "I will be telling him . . ."

"You will not!" Enid said. Her voice came clipped, taking command. "You will go in the front room, all of you. I will see to this."

"But, Mom . . ."

"Go! Put the television on. Act ordinary. Go on. Quick!"

"Come on, Grandad," Gwyneth said.

Enid waited in the storm of Blod's barking until they were gone and the music of the television came. Until the old man swore and Blod yelped and there was comparative silence. She alone with only the door between her and the night. Snug they were now, settled nicely when the man knocked again. Enid drew back the bolts to let him in.

He did not wait to be asked. He stepped past her into the kitchen with a quick good evening, and she was annoyed with him. The door jammed on the flagstones and would not shut. Her knuckles bruised on the wall as she forced it.

Captain Willoughby-Smythe had made himself at home. His cap and gloves were placed neatly on the table and he was poring over the survey map. The knapsack was at his feet. He did not look at her. He traced a pencil route over the mountains.

"Going hiking?"

"It is the school holidays," Enid said primly as she filled the kettle. "Rhys is going hiking with a friend of his."

"Bit out of date, this map, isn't it? Nineteen fifty-one?"

"Mountains don't change," Enid said. "Tea?"

"Yes, please."

He left the map, prowled, a man in a cage of light, filling the room with his presence. He seemed to be looking for something, casually searching the spaces between the clock and the tea caddy, between the letter rack and the vase where the pens are kept. He touched things, idly examined a tube of bronze lipstick, a bottle of sheep drench, a jar of hand cream. Searching, he was, and Enid grew more and more angry.

"If you tell me what you're looking for, maybe I'll tell you where to find it!"

"I'm not sure what I'm looking for," he said.

"The pound notes are stowed under my mattress!"

"Where do you keep the aspirins?" he asked.

He opened the cupboard.

Enid slammed the teacups on the table. "You have absolutely no right!"

"No," he agreed coolly.

"No right to walk in here prying into other people's things!"

"Unfortunately, it is sometimes necessary."

"Get out of my house!" Enid said savagely.

He turned to her, closed the cupboard door. In his hand was a small bottle of pills.

"What's this?" he asked her.

Enid sat on the edge of the chair. She could feel

herself crumbling. She did not know what to do about this man, how to combat his ruthless calm, defy his knowledge. Part of her screamed hate for him, part of her wanted to turn to him, clutch and cling. But she was Welsh-born and stubborn like her father. She would not give way that easily and he would not trap her with his sly English words. It was morphine written on the label.

"Morphine," Enid said grimly. "As prescribed by the doctor."

"For your father?"

His cold gray eyes dared her to lie.

"No," Enid said. "Not for my father."

The captain nodded. "No," he repeated as he placed the bottle gently on the table. "Not for your father, because there's nothing wrong with your father, is there? You lied, you see, and I checked with my men. Old men with bronchial pneumonia don't go four times to the outside lavatory, mend the hinges of the fowl coop, or take constitutionals on the lower slopes of a mountain."

"It's a pity you've nothing better to do than count the number of times people use the lavatory!"

"It's a pity you didn't tell me the truth in the first place," he said levelly.

"What truth?" Enid snapped.

"That he's here, in this house."

Enid did not confirm or deny, but her eyes made him certain, staring at him from a face without color. Then she bent her head. He had beaten her. He was an official from the English army and she could have nothing to say to him. She covered her face with her hands. She did not know how to cope anymore. She couldn't tell him Erlich was not here. He knew.

She sat there, unmoving. The room was quiet. From far away she heard the television voices, and nearer she heard the stairs creak. The man did not speak to her. When the kettle boiled he moved to make the tea and then again she was locked with him in the silence. She thought it would go on all night, but after a while he touched her shoulder, the pressure of his hand was firm and comforting.

"Come on," he said gently.

The splits between her fingers showed her the light, showed her the tea he was offering.

"Drink it," he said. "It will make you feel better."

It spilled hot over her hands and she was shaking. But it was strong and reviving and he had remembered she didn't take sugar. She tried not to notice him but he was tall beside her, leaning against the bar of the stove, watching her, disconcerting.

"Why didn't you tell me?" he asked her.

"How could I?"

"You could have trusted me."

"You were the last person!"

"I have dealt with situations like this before, you know."

"What situations?"

He sighed. "Do you want me to spell it out for you? He is here, in this house. Fox on the run hides his trail in the water. He took to the stream. We might never have known, but you were not thinking straight, nor was Rhys. So now we do know. We have found traces of his blood in your barn. He's hurt and cornered and dangerous, and he's here. I suppose he's holding your daughter as hostage?"

"What?" Enid whispered.

"I thought so," the captain said grimly. "I guessed that was why you wouldn't talk, why Dr. Price-Jones made a false statement. But there's no point in your keeping silent now. He must know I'm here. He must know who I am and what I represent. So why don't you tell me?"

Enid stared at him.

"Don't you see?" he said.

She saw, but she did not quite believe.

"You're not on your own anymore," he said. "You don't have to cope alone. I'm here. I'm empowered to make a deal with him."

Enid wanted to laugh, wildly, madly, fill the light with her laughter . . . because he had no idea . . . because Erlich was gold and gentle and the danger was not from him. He was the danger . . . Captain Willoughby-Smythe, and he could no more make a deal with Erlich than he could with the Mawrrhyn. They were both beyond human bargaining . . . beautiful, terrible, powerful forces . . . a star lord and a mountain, wild and uncontainable, and free. Softly Enid started to laugh.

"You don't understand!"

He didn't begin to understand.

From the black space of the doorway a trigger clicked. The old man's rabbiting gun was leveled at his head.

"There's no deal," Rhys said. "So get your hands up."

20

If Enid had ever lost control, she did not show it. It all seemed natural somehow. Natural the grim determination on Gwyneth's face, the menace of the gun barrel, like a scene in a drama they had all rehearsed before. She knew what to do without Rhys telling her.

Captain Willoughby-Smythe stood perfectly still, shocked and disbelieving, with his arms half raised. Keeping open the line of fire, Enid moved to search him. She felt his breath brushing her face, the nearness of his eyes. She felt the uncomfortable warmth of his closeness, the warmth of their physical contact as she groped under his jacket for the black revolver he kept there. Then she too had a gun in her hand.

"I am sorry," said Enid. "But sit down, please."

His anger was quiet and terrible.

"What do you think you're doing?"

"Sit down!" Rhys said.

"And if I don't, will you shoot me?"

"Please," said Enid. "There is enough hurt without that."

"Are you all mad, or something?"

"Or something," said Rhys. "So do what you're told."

He obeyed quite suddenly, as if he had consciously decided to, not because he was threatened. He allowed himself to be tied to the chair. And his eyes were full of scorn as Gwyneth bound his wrists tight behind him with baling twine, and tied his ankles to the struts. Finally Enid put the revolver on the table and Rhys lowered the gun.

"You won't get away with it, of course."

"No," said Rhys. "We don't expect to. Not indefinitely."

"Just long enough," said Gwyneth.

"Long enough for him to get clear?"

"That's right," Rhys said calmly.

"You'd better tell him to hurry, then."

"Why?"

"My driver is outside," said Captain Willoughby-Smythe. "And he knows his orders."

They looked at each other.

In Gwyneth came a feeling of panic.

"Now what'll we do? We'll have to tie *him* up too!"

"You expect me to go through all this again?" Rhys asked.

"You heard him! Orders, he said!"

"And orders can be changed," Enid murmured.

She was quite calm. She took off her dirty apron and draped it over the chair.

"What are you going to do?" Gwyneth asked her.

Enid didn't answer. She went quickly upstairs. They heard her moving around the rooms, her footsteps on the floorboards. They heard the wardrobe door creak open and shut, the sound of drawers in Gwyneth's room. The waiting grew tense.

"What's she doing?" Gwyneth said.

"How would I know?" Rhys retorted.

"She can't change army orders!"

"So tell *her*, not me!"

Captain Willoughby-Smythe was smiling sardonically.

But Enid had changed herself.

She was not middle-aged and dowdy anymore. She was wearing a black low-cut sweater, and Gwyneth's tight, flared trousers clung to the shape of her body. They had never seen her looking like that before. There was rouge on her cheeks and her eyes were brilliant, dark and accentuated with mascara. A pair of gold earrings jangled. Gwyneth stared at her, silently disapproving.

"What are you doing, Mom?" Rhys asked curiously.

"I am going to have a word with that driver," Enid said.

"Looking like that!" said Gwyneth.

"What's wrong with it?"

Gwyneth didn't need to tell her. Enid knew what she was looking like and so did Captain Willoughby-Smythe. He was watching her and his lips were tight with the same disapproval. Enid pulled the sweater down tight over the contours of her bust. The neckline plunged over her naked skin.

"Will I do?" she asked him.

He looked away and didn't answer her.

Enid nodded. She would do very well.

She went alone out into the night. Pitch-black was the sky, without a star, and the wind was cold. She clutched her arms, clutched the scent of her own perfume, and went down the long yard to the road. She could see the Land-Rover parked by the gate, with its headlights on dim. She was not nervous. She had done worse things than this in her time, once in a Cardiff nightclub without even thinking.

She let the gate swing open behind her, passed like a shadow through the pale beams of light. The man behind the wheel was watching her and he must have guessed she was coming for him. The door swung open and the inside light came on. Enid smiled, bent down to talk to him.

"You are waiting for the captain?"

"What's wrong?"

"Nothing. He has changed his mind, that's all."

"Changed his mind?"

"Yes. There is no need for you to wait. He is staying."

The soldier frowned at her. "You're Mrs. Williams, aren't you?"

"That's right," Enid said.

"What d'you mean . . . staying?"

He was not seeing, the young soldier in his black beret, not understanding what she meant. And Enid had not wanted to say this, but she had no other choice.

"Staying," she emphasized. "With me . . . for the night. Got it?"

The soldier glanced at her, quick and sharp, for the first time seeing her as a woman, a woman mature and attractive in her black seductive clothes. He had got it. The knowledge was there in his eyes.

"Oh," he said heavily.

"That's all right," Enid said as she turned to go.

But it was not all right.

"Just a minute," the soldier said quickly.

He was worried. He pushed his beret to the back of his head and scratched his forehead. He stared into the dark beyond the window as if he did not know what to

say. Finally he pounded his fist on the steering wheel
and turned to her.

"You realize there's a whole army unit and half the
police force on standby!"

"Well, that's not my fault," Enid said.

"No," said the soldier. "But it's his! He can't go off
duty just like that! I mean . . . who's going to tell them?
Me?"

"You would rather he came and told you himself?"

"No. Hell . . . I don't know. This just isn't like
him."

Enid nodded. "I'll tell him to come himself."

"No . . . it's all right . . . I mean . . . if that's what
he said. I can tell them it's off and he made a mistake.
But you can tell him . . . I'm not taking the rap. He'll
have to do his own explaining."

"I'll tell him," Enid promised.

"He'll be with you if he's needed?"

"Yes."

The soldier nodded, started the engine. "Have a
nice time," he said.

She turned to go in and he drove past her up the
lane. There would be no more trouble. The gate
clanged shut. She felt low, and cheap, and shabby.
She had made a lie by implication and Captain
Willoughby-Smythe would not thank her. The smut on
his reputation was one more thing she could add to
Erlich's price.

"He's gone," she said as she entered the kitchen.

Rhys and Gwyneth did not ask how or why, and
Captain Willoughby-Smythe already knew. She waited
for his disgust but it did not come. In his eyes there
was nothing more than the struggle to understand her.

"Why?" he asked her. "In God's name, why?"

"I could think of no other way," Enid said.

"That's no answer."

"We had to do something!"

"But why?"

"It's none of your business," Gwyneth said.

"Isn't it?" The captain turned to her. "You've trussed me up like a chicken, threatened a ranking officer at gunpoint, and now you tell me it's none of my business. Don't I have a right to know why? Why you're holding me? Why you're all risking your necks to let him escape? You can go to jail for this! Is he worth that much to you? Is he?"

They could not tell him how much Erlich was worth. Not in words could they hope to make him understand. But without his understanding they would all be condemned.

"Fetch him, Gwyneth," Rhys said quietly.

"Why? It's not his fault! He's done nothing!"

"Fetch him!"

Gwyneth went muttering through the dark hallway, into the gunfight of the television, the stagnance of Granny Thomas' funeral parlor. She didn't see why Erlich should answer for what they'd done. She didn't see why he should stand trial.

Shapeless and muffled in Gwyneth's duffel coat, Erlich crouched over the fire, with the old man beside him and Blod at his feet. Perhaps for the last time Gwyneth would see him with his golden grace, beautiful and bright, before he was gone, leaving her empty, and the house empty, and only the mountains outside. And of course he was worth it. It was worth everything to know he would go on existing somewhere, free and unquestionable. But that stupid man wouldn't see it.

The television blared, "You're going to die for this, Coogan. You're going to die."

Wind rattled the loose window frame.

"You're wanted in the kitchen," Gwyneth said. The old man looked around. "Going, are we?"

"Not you," said Gwyneth. "Erlich."

Erlich stiffened. "Why?"

"Yes," said Gwyneth. "That's what *he* wants to know."

And from the television came the final gunshot.

He stood alone, prey in the eyes of the hunter, his face white below the unshaded light. Slowly his fists clenched and unclenched. His life was worth no more no less than any other life. His freedom no more no less than any other freedom. He was not special, not unique. There were others like himself and they did not claim to be a divine breed. Erlich could not claim to be the reason. He could not stand as justification for what Rhys and Enid had done. He could not say to this bound, uniformed man: Whatever you suffer, they suffer, I am worth it. He was not that arrogant.

His head lifted proudly.

"What do you want me to say?"

He did not have to say anything. He was a star lord with his pale gold hair. A being who was proud and beautiful, belonging to a different destiny from theirs. His quiet power seemed to fill the room. His eyes were the feel of chords, blue striking deep down in the soul of them. There was no price for him. He was among all other priceless things, belonging to no one, belonging to all, like music, like art, like a poet's words. He could give nothing more, just a vision of himself and his kind, a dream of the universe, a glimpse of hope among the gray, sad cities of the planet earth.

Captain Willoughby-Smythe was not immune.

"What do I say to you?" Erlich asked him.

"Nothing," the man said quietly.

"You are enough," Enid said. "On your own."

"You can put your hat back on," Rhys said gruffly.

"But I thought . . ."

"You can go," Gwyneth said. "It is all done now. There is nothing more." She put the bottle of tablets in his pocket. "Two, if you need them. Don't forget."

"But . . ."

"You want to stay for Christmas?" Rhys asked him.

"No."

"So come on then." Rhys picked up the knapsack. "Grandad! We're off!"

"Good luck," Captain Willoughby-Smythe said softly.

It was so quick, so sudden.

The hallway filled with their departing shadows, with Blod's claws on the stone among the maze of their legs. The outside door opened in a blast of blackness and the night swallowed them, slowly, the sound of their voices, their shapes, their existence. What remained behind them was the husk of the house, a drained emptiness.

"No!" Gwyneth cried as Enid went to shut the door.

"There is nothing more we can do," Enid said firmly.

"How can you bear it?"

"You just do," said Enid.

"It's all right for you!" Gwyneth howled. "It's only Rhys and Grandad, and they're coming back."

Enid shut the door. It was all right for her. But down inside her was a hollow pain and a numbness, a grief that would never be filled. She wished she could cry like Gwyneth.

21

Rhys waited with the darkness like a wall against his eyes. Waited as it split into shades of earth and sky, the splash of white on Blod's paws, the solid outline of the mountains up ahead. Then he was on the track with the loose stone slipping under his feet and Blod walking quietly beside him. And the stream was a black gash down in the gully to the left of him, the sound of it drowning the old man and Erlich, who came behind.

The track ended at the head of the valley by the ruins of a cottage, dung-filled rooms that the sheep used. In the lee of a wall Rhys waited, and the mountains encircled him, the arms of the Mawrrhyn joining the Brechin, black and high, towering with menace.

"You don't scare me, lady," Rhys said.

They had come less than a mile but already Erlich was in pain. His breathing was harsh. His heart beat the bruises of his ribs.

"Make it, will you?"

"I'll make it," Erlich said, gasping.

"Only we start climbing now, see."

"Where?"

"Up there. So if you want to take a rest . . ."

Erlich glanced, then moved to sit in an alcove of a wall that had once been a window. He drew up his legs and rested his head on his knees. He looked beaten. As if the sight of the Mawrrhyn's steepness had sapped the last of his strength.

"We're not going up there?"

"Yes, unfortunately."

"That wasn't the way I came."

"No? Which way did you come, then?"

"Over there," said Erlich, flapping his hand.

"Brechin," said Hywel Thomas.

"It's much easier, surely?"

"Aye, but there's soldiers and dogs over Brechin, boyo."

"Which is why we're going over the Mawrrhyn," Rhys said.

Erlich lifted his head. In the pale, strange light of his face, his expression was bitter. "Take me over that mountain," he said, "and someone will pay . . . you and everyone concerning you . . . and the ones who live will be the ones who regret it."

It was very quiet in the deep well of the valley. Somewhere in the darkness a stone fell.

Rhys licked the dry salt sores on his lips. "What are you saying?"

Erlich shook his head. "I'm not sure. I just say it. I just feel it. There's a power up there, waiting for me, knowing I am here. I can't cross it because I can't pay . . . because I've paid already with my ship and my power and I have nothing left to give. I cannot serve time that is meaningless."

Rhys stared up at the sheer, dark rising.

"Power? Up there?"

"Mawrrhyn," said Hywel Thomas grimly. "Her, he is meaning."

"A sheep-ravaged mountain? Power?"

"You mind her, boyo. And you mind what he says."

Rhys sat with Blod at his feet.

He didn't believe. He didn't want to believe.

"What power?"

Clouds hung dark before the face of the moon and Erlich began talking. His voice was soft, speaking to no person, speaking to the world out beyond the valley, words in the wind, in the black rushing water. But his eyes burned into Rhys like cold blue flames.

He said there were places on this earth where his kind did not go, tracts of the sea and land, places with atmospheres where they did not trespass, powers which they did not disturb. He did not know why or what they were, only that they were there, had always been there.

And in the olden days men also recognized these places, endowed them with spirits, fiends and trolls, nymphs of the waters, oreads of the mountains, strange or terrible creatures to be worshiped or avoided. Their shapes were lost now, gone into myth and legend, but something remained, some power of them still in the places where they existed, in the areas marked red on Erlich's chart. And perhaps in the depths of the human mind there was a latent memory, a fear of the banshee wailing in the Irish bogs, the wild, cruel, bittersweet song of a Siren on some remote, sea-beaten shore. They were not dead, these powers of the earth. Not banished. They lurked still in the shadow lands, crossed and recrossed through the doorways of their own dimensions.

"And there is a power in this mountain," Erlich said.

"Aye," Hywel Thomas said with a growl. "Mawr-rhyn."

"Maureen," Erlich said carefully, "She is a grid number on a map and we do not cross her. We use the flight path over the other mountains to the north. But I came this way . . . and she knew."

Rhys took a deep breath.

"Are you telling me that a lump of glaciated granite can hook an interstellar flying machine out of her airspace and smash it?"

"Yes. I am telling you."

"It was an accident, man!"

"It was intentional."

"A fault in the engine."

"The on-board computer would have registered."

"Your navigation up the spout!"

"It was her," Erlich insisted. "Maureen, as you call her."

"Mawr-rhyn!"

Rhys clutched his head.

"All right . . . allowing that . . . allowing it was her . . . why should she? What possible reason could she have?"

"She is not needing a reason," Hywel Thomas said.

"All things need reason!"

"Then there is little enough of it in this world."

"Whose fault is that? Men and governments! Not mountains!"

"Erlich sighed. "I don't know her reasons . . . but I sense . . . power disturbs power. Isn't that true anyway? Disturb the balance, and what happens? Things strike back . . . men against governments . . . nature against man . . . she against me."

"But why? Why you?"

"Because my power is not like hers?" Erlich guessed. "I use pure and applied science, but what does she use? Mysticism! Once we scorned it as rubbish, but eons ago we came to accept that there were some things we could not understand, forces that defied science. She and I . . . we could destroy each other . . . because we cannot ever understand. I cannot ever understand her, yet I feel she is where I am. Like me, she is ageless. Like me she has conquered time and space, but in some other, different way. I think she could even send me home, if only I could ask her."

"Then why don't you!" Rhys said. "Save us all a seven-mile walk!"

"If he would ask help from the Mawrrhyn he must pay her price," Hywel Thomas said darkly. "And he has already told you he cannot pay. He cannot pay, see? And she is cruel and not giving, even unto men."

Rhys stood up.

"So what's she want then? New pence or sacrifice? There's one of our sheep gone rotten down by the lake and the Severn Bridge toll fee is twelve pence. She can have both . . . mutton and money!" He felt in his pocket. Loose coins fell among the stones as he flung them. "One week's pocket money! The price of a crossing ! I've paid!"

Erlich didn't move.

Rhys turned to him, exasperated. "It's not logic! Look you . . . there she is! Grandad's been walking over her for seventy-five years with hobnail boots on. Coachloads of tourists drop litter on her. Blod shits on her, and I've climbed her a few hundred times. Nothing happens. Nothing's ever happened. Nothing's going to happen. She's stone-cold dead! Slate and bedrock! She wouldn't notice a bulldozer going over her, let alone you. So you may as well come on."

The wind whined among the crags of the Mawrrhyn, flickered the flames of Erlich's eyes.

"I've told you," he said softly.

"And I've listened."

"Listened but not heard," the old man muttered.

"If I heard," said Rhys, "does it change what we have to do?"

He shouldered the knapsack.

"There's no other way," he said relentlessly. "So I'm going . . . up over the Mawrrhyn. You got three choices, Erlich. Go back home and let the English army captain sling you in jail. Go over the Brechin and the dogs will get you. Or follow me. Unless you want to stay here all night exchanging fairy stories with Grandad and die of exposure. It's up to you. Come on, Blod."

He left them, cut from the track to the mountain, and his feet sank silently in wet grass and bog moss. The bottoms of his jeans flapped sodden around his legs. He should have worn higher boots. He should have followed Blod's white blaze around the drier places. She was waiting for him, patient among the first outcrop of rock, her eyes glinting with dark. Animals sensed things, but Blod had no fear. And there was nothing up there, no power, no person, no Valkyrie or mountain lady. Only wind-beaten rocks and Welsh superstition. Rhys started to climb and he heard Erlich and the old man follow.

"Do your worst, Mawrrhyn," Rhys said softly.

The only power she had fell behind him in a black drop, and his boots struck sparks on the stones. It was easy.

But it was not easy for Erlich and Hywel Thomas. It was a climb in the black night up tortuous sheep paths, along narrow ledges, and across the great bare slopes of scree. It was exertion of sense and muscle that set the old man panting and the barbed pain striking in Erlich's ribs. They didn't talk much. They had neither room nor breath for talk.

Up and up the Mawrrhyn rose without rest or relief. A grueling place. The blackness of the valley grew deep and perilous, like a chasm yawning beneath, and Erlich's pain grew worse, worse with every breath, every step, every heaving effort. He couldn't make it, couldn't go on. He clung to a boulder, rested his head. Through the crook of his arm he could see the lights of Llanysted far below and far away. He could feel the nearness of the sky over him. But the mountain held him, the black unbearable pain that stabbed and twisted and crushed.

"I can't," Erlich moaned. "Not anymore I can't."

There was no one to see his defeat, his end on the outpost planet billions of miles from home. There was only an old man speaking words in a language Erlich could no longer strain to understand. And then another voice came, young and urgent, railing him without pity. He wanted to lie down but they would not let him. They dragged him bodily up and over the edge. Hauled him into a space onto nowhere where the fists of the wind beat his face before he was allowed to lie still.

Rhys caught his breath, stared at him, a star lord on the dirty earth.

"Done for, he is," said Hywel Thomas, panting, as he sank on a stone.

"He can't be!"

"Had it, boyo. Same as me."

"There's six more miles!"

The old man coughed.

"That was the last mile he will ever walk in this world."

22

"You won't make it, will you?" Rhys asked quietly.

Erlich closed his eyes.

"No," said Rhys. "You won't make it."

It was a physical fact. The sound in his lungs was thick and rasping, like a death rattle. He had no strength left, not even to talk, and there was nothing Rhys could do for him. He had fed him hot soup and morphine tablets, but the fact remained. Hywel Thomas was right. Erlich wouldn't be walking seven rough miles to Cwmvanwy. He wouldn't be walking anywhere. He was done for. Rhys covered him with the groundsheet and turned away.

Damp in the wind set the old man coughing. They were all done for.

On the high summit of the Mawrrhyn, Rhys sat. The world was dark down beneath him, the lights of the farmhouse yellow in the valley. And over on the

Brechin were the soldiers, with their lighted tents, guns, and dogs, and arc lights. Just this one night they had. One night before Enid let Willoughby-Smythe go free. And they would spend it trapped on a bare mountain, going neither forward nor back. Rhys was brooding and bitter. Cold seeped through his anorak. The wind cried among the crags. It was a black, desolate place and it had beaten him.

"What can you do?" Rhys asked. "Against all of this?"

The old man coughed, spat phlegm among the rocks. Coughed, spat, coughed. He couldn't answer. There was no answer. No way out.

Into her world, Enid had said, and for that we must pay.

"How?" Rhys asked. "Just answer me that, will you?"

And this *was* her world, stretching before and after time. Moors and mountains and valleys going on and on while men lived and died. He would give her that much. Give her the vast, windswept reaches, the territory of rock and bog, the gorse brakes and the heather. But he would not give her halls in a hollow mountain, some fey power, and a woman's form. If she had world and power it was explainable in logical terms. It was not a load of myths cooked up by the locals.

But Erlich wasn't stupid. He wasn't stupid enough to believe in fairies. But he believed in something. Power, he said, marked red on a chart drawn by experts more expert than any scientist on this earth. There were tracts of sea and land where his kind did not go. Places that were wild and dangerous. He wasn't stupid and he wasn't lying. There *was* something here. There was *something*

"What?" said Rhys.

What is in the dark, brooding rocks and the jagged skyline?

"Some kind of elemental force? A magnetic influx? Atmospheric disturbances? Some kind of gravitational whirlpool that dragged him down?"

Blod came, thrust her face between his knees, looked up at him, and whined. He fondled her ears.

"What is it, Blod? There's got to be something."

"Aye," the old man wheezed. "There is something, right enough. But you will not find it thinkingly with maths and physics and all them things. She is not for people's understanding."

"Power, Erlich said."

"And it is power he is not understanding any more than you."

"You got to be born simple, I suppose? Like Morgan, or Thomas, or Jones?"

"You got to learn respect, boyo!" Hywel Thomas said roughly.

"Respect for what?"

"Respect like he has learned for things he does not understand. He respects that they are so and does not question. You would do good to follow him."

Rhys frowned.

Don't question. Don't ask why dozens of boats and planes went missing in one triangle of ocean off the coast of Bermuda. Why voodoo happened. Why the Irish saw leprechauns and why Dafydd Jones' nephew had disappeared on the moors without trace. Don't ask questions, but it's not all due to bog and wind and freak currents.

Rhys stared around him.

Mawrrhyn. Her breath was cold, her spirit roaming. She was here in the moods of earth and stone, in the wind's whine and the cliff fall. She was the rock-scarred age of this place. The bleak barren beauty of summer days. The stark gray cruelty of winter. She was the flower of the bog myrtle, the claws of the dung beetle, the scabbed gray flakes of lichen, the leaf and the thorn. She was here, now, always, waiting in the darkness for her price.

Nature had a way of hitting back.

And the Mawrrhyn had struck his ship from the sky, because his power was not like hers. To her, Erlich was destruction on a scale hardly begun on earth. He was the power of concrete and atom bombs, exhausts spewing carbon monoxide factory waste, plastic, poison, and pollution. He was mechanized science in its final terrifying form, and the Mawrrhyn knew. Erlich could build cities from her rubble, dams across her streams, cabbage where the sundew grew. He could destroy her utterly.

"Only he wouldn't," Rhys reasoned. "Erlich wouldn't do that. He wouldn't destroy her. He wouldn't destroy anything. It's us, not him! He's learned respect, but we threaten. He's not part of the Gwent Water Board. It's not even his world. All he wants is to leave her alone."

"That is what he was telling you, boyo. It is a bit late now for the listening."

"I brought him here," Rhys said. "I made him come."

"Aye."

"What'll we do, then?"

"We will be' paying for the mistake," the old man said calmly.

Paying.

Death by exposure. Rhys licked the blood from his cracked lips. A scud of rain lashed his back. The wind was freezing, and Erlich lay motionless on the bare ground. They could go home if it weren't for him.

But they couldn't leave him up here to die alone. It wasn't human.

Blod whined, restless, wanting to move on.

Rhys reached for her, comfort perhaps, comfort for himself in the blind, wet dark. His hands in her fur groped for the warmth, Blod drawn close to him, back like she had never been gone, knowing his need. Blod never questioned. She just loved and accepted. Loved. Licked his hands and his face and his hair. And he clung to her like she was the last thing on earth, like this was the last time he would ever love Blod. And it was not rain, it was sleet matting her fur and freezing.

The Mawrrhyn had no mercy.

Rhys pushed Blod away. He was quite numb, even his mind. But the night was sharp and in focus. A drift of smoke from the old man's pipe blew in his face. Through torn clouds a pale trace of moonlight glittered on wet stones, glittered on the rain shafts of the sky. They did not all need to die.

"Best get back, Grandad," Rhys said.

"Aye."

"No point in you getting soaked."

"Nope."

"Nothing you can do anyway."

"Nope."

"We'll work something out, me and him."

"Aye."

Hywel Thomas banged out his pipe on the rock. Rich red sparks flew in the wind and were instantly extinguished. He put the pipe in his pocket. He was not hurrying. He had lived slow all his life and the end would not change him.

"He is her kind," said Hywel Thomas. "Remember that."

"All right," said Rhys without understanding.

"They are not meaning to be cruel. It is just their way."

The old man heaved himself up with his stick. "Well, Blodwyn. Ready, are we?" Blod came to him, tail wagging. "We will be getting back, girlie, you and me."

She wined, dark-eyed and eager.

"They are not needing the likes of us anymore."

"Grandad," said Rhys.

"Aye?"

"You'll tell Mom, will you?"

Hywel Thomas nodded. He did not ask what he must tell or what Rhys would do. He shuffled slowly away into the black of the night, an old man and his dog, going back down the mountain, going home. He did not say good-bye. Rhys swallowed down the lump in his throat and turned to face the dark other direction.

The blown sleet slashed him.

He is her kind, remember that, Grandad had said.

"Wake up!"

Erlich groaned as Rhys shook him.

"Wake up! You can't just lie there! We got to do something!"

He was hauled upright, swaying as he stood and clutching Rhys for support. His face was drugged white. His blue eyes were glazed. His pale hair blown by the wind, drenched by the icy rain. Dull pain numbed him.

"We got to get out of here!" Rhys howled.

His words were ripped from his mouth and spun away into darkness. Like a great torn wing, the ground-sheet flapped. Over the ridge a lamb cried for its mother, and the swollen stream poured down the valley. The wind was wild and savage and beating him as he dragged Erlich to the shelter of a boulder.

"You hearing me?" Rhys asked.

"Yes," Erlich muttered.

"We got to do something."

"What?"

"Power, you said. Her power. You got to use it."

Erlich looked at him, quick and sharp.

The wind screamed.

"Do you know what you're saying?" Erlich asked.

"Yes," said Rhys. "If there's one chance in hell, it's worth taking. Death is no use to her. She wants life . . . one of us . . . you go . . . I pay . . . no point the other way . . . go on! I'm your price."

Everything went still.

The wind dropped and there was silence, a pause before movement and a blue calm in Erlich's eyes. Before him on the flank of the Mawrrhyn was a burned black circle, and all among the grass and rocks were the minute phosphorescent glints of metal. Far away and small below, the hidden moonlight touched the dark waters of the lake. Erlich had jumped into the lake, jumped from a stricken spacecraft, and lived. Someone he did not question had not intended him to die.

It will take more than you, or I, or Rhys, or that silly old man, to change what will be, Enid had said.

Erlich looked up. Between the broken clouds shone a single star. Eridani Epsilon . . . pale and small and infinitely distant. The air was sharp with his longing. Rhys was the price and Erlich would not refuse. It was meant to be this way.

Rhys waited. Inside him there was no more fight. He had acknowledged a power he did not understand. The Mawrrhyn took him gently. One flake of snow touched his face, then another. And everywhere the snow was falling, white in the sky, white on the ground, white on Erlich's hair. White, gentle, surrendering. You couldn't go against a mountain if you were not her kind.

But Erlich was her kind. Hers like Hywel Thomas said he was. Paid for with a life, he was, but in the blue of his eyes there was no emotion. Clear as jewels they were, and containing a cold equal to any cold the Mawrrhyn could show. Like her he was beautiful. Like her he was cruel. There was no mercy.

"I can't thank you," Erlich whispered.

"No."

"But I will remember."

"Just get on with it."

"One day . . ."

"Yes," said Rhys. "All right . . . one day . . . sometime . . . I know . . . it'll still be here . . . so will you . . . and you won't forget. It doesn't matter. Just get on with it."

Erlich turned to the mountain.

He spoke in a language Rhys did not know, words he could not understand. Words so old that the meaning was lost down in time, but the Mawrrhyn remembered. Soft as a murmuring Erlich spoke, slow like a chant until the syllables became one continuous sound, almost music. High it rose, and wild, like wing beats or fire, reaching up through the snow-flying sky, reaching down into earth until the black rocks echoed it and the ground started to tremble. Stones fell. Scree slipped with a noise of thunder. Somewhere a dog howled and an old man screamed, but Rhys could not heed them. There was only the magic gripping his guts, only the Mawrrhyn answering Erlich's call.

Slowly and silently and down below, a door opened in the mountainside, and a strange green light flowed out.

Powers, Erlich had said. Powers he knew nothing about. Doorways into other dimensions.

Rhys didn't hesitate. One chance in hell and this was it. He knew it wouldn't last long. But Erlich had used the last strength he had. Rhys half-carried, half-dragged him, down over rocks and scree. The snow blinded him but the door stayed open, and the light guided him like a beacon. Then at last he was inside, bathed in a green warmth, in a cave without dark or cold or fear. He was out of the night and out of the world. He need never worry again. In a mixture of joy and relief, Rhys looked back.

There was a rock door slowly closing behind him, and beyond it was Blod.

Blod . . . she had come to fetch him back. She was whining, fast and desperate. Her claws scrabbled the rock. Her crying was terrible and urgent, begging him to come. And it all crashed in on him . . . Erlich's magic and the old man's scream, Enid, Gwyneth, and home. He had to get out. Hywel Thomas was hurt and Blod wanted help. There was no question.

Rhys dumped Erlich's body, hurled himself at the opening. But he was not quick enough. His fingers clawed at a crack of stone and then dropped.

That brown crying love in Blod's eyes was the last thing Rhys saw before the door to the Mawrrhyn shut.

23

Gwyneth cried and slept.

She woke in the early hours of morning. She was stiff and cold. She had been sleeping on top of the bed with her clothes on. The house was very quiet, no sound, no movement. Only the wind down the chimney, only a dog howling sadly some distance away. Gwyneth turned her head. The alarm clock said ten past three and she had forgotten to draw the curtains. There was a light outside, pale and strange. A whiteness more eerie than moonlight. She groped for her slippers under the bed and went to the window.

It was snow. Snow lying thick on the ground, white on the roofs of the outbuildings, and moonlight clear as day. She could see the Mawrrhyn rising high and ghostly over the black gash of the valley, and the sky was brilliant with stars. Gwyneth shivered. It was all frozen and beautiful. Faint frosty ferns formed on the window glass and melted under her breath. The stars compelled her to look.

Glorious, they were. White and gold like Erlich's hair. Through the vast, silent distance they had called her out of sleep. She wanted to go, out into the night and the snow. She wanted to stand in the wind song under the stars and bear witness. Something told her, something said . . . if she dodn't go she would regret it . . . she would spend the rest of her life and never know.

Quickly and quietly Gwyneth crept downstairs. There was a light on in the kitchen. She opened the door.

"Mom?" Gwyneth said softly.

Captain Willoughby-Smythe was asleep, still tied to the chair, and Enid sat with the rifle in her lap. She was staring at some spot among the mess on the mantel-shelf, but she was not seeing. She had gone vacant into a trance where the small clock ticked the seconds and the hall clock struck the hours but time itself had no real meaning.

"Mom!" Gwyneth said sharply.

Captain Willoughby-Smythe raised his head. "She won't hear you."

"She doesn't want to. How long's she been sitting like that?"

"Almost as long as I've been sitting like this."

"She used to get like this with our dad," Gwyneth said. "She'd go days sometimes. Walk around the house like a zombie and not say a word. I thought all that was over when we came here. Where's Grandad?"

"Your grandfather has not come home," the captain said.

When Enid couldn't cope she withdrew. It's all right for you! Gwyneth had howled. It's only Rhys and

Grandad, and they're coming back. But Hywel Thomas hadn't come back. Gwyneth stood perfectly still in the warm bright room. He was stubborn and cantankerous but he'd never once made her feel unwanted. Like the mountains, he was, old and dependable, giving her a home. He should have been back hours ago but Enid stared into space with unseeing eyes and Gwyneth did not know what to do.

"Will you untie me please."

The man's voice reached her and she did not think. She took a knife from the drawer and sawed through the string that bound his wrists. She was slow and fumbling. The knife was blunt and tears blurred her vision. The strands of baling twine frayed and broke, and she bent to cut the cords around his ankles. Hair fell across her eyes and she sniffed.

"Give it to me," he said quietly.

He took the knife from her hand. He was free in a single stroke and pocketing his revolver.

Gwyneth sat on the mat, useless.

"Make your mother some tea," he said. "I have to go outside."

He went for the lavatory and Gwyneth wiped her nose on her cardigan. Instincts of function went on no matter what, and there wasn't much time. She filled the kettle from the scullery pump, but the fire was choked with dead ash. Ashes to ashes. It was only Grandad. Only an old man who had already lived his life. She dashed her hand across her eyes and reached for the poker. Dust blew in clouds. Useless.

He took over, the English army captain. His wrists were strong and hairy. He was quiet and efficient, with his black military mustache. He wasn't anyone's fancy man. There was ash on his uniform and soot on his hands, but his eyes were gray and kind and Gwyneth was glad he was there. He sent her for kindling and coaxed the fire to burn. Pale fresh flames leaped upward and he put the kettle on to boil. And all the time Enid sat, seeing and not seeing.

"Mom knows about Grandad," Gwyneth said.

"Yes, I'm afraid so."

"There's still a chance though, isn't there?"

"It's been snowing."

"Yes, I know. I saw from upstairs."

"Then there's not much chance, is there?"

"Grandad's known mountains all his life."

"And he's an old man. An old man with a wheezy chest who has been missing for nine hours. There are subzero temperatures up on those mountains. Almost no chance, I'd say. And not much of a chance for Rhys, unless your golden-haired boy can work miracles."

They were standing together by the stove, man and girl. For the first time they looked at each other.

"Can he?" the captain asked her.

"What?"

"Work miracles?"

"He wouldn't let Rhys die," Gwyneth said slowly. "I know that much. If he's alive, then Rhys is also alive."

"And if he's dead?"

Gwyneth shook her head. "He's not dead."

"How can you tell?"

"I can't. Something tells *me*. Erlich's alive."

"Telepathy?"

"I don't know. It's a feeling. I know he's alive. And if we go outside we'll know for sure. I don't know how we'll know, but something is going to happen. It will happen just once and never again, and we have to see it. You can know and not know, but if you actually see something then you're certain you know. Does that sound crazy?"

"It sounds like everything else that doesn't bear questioning," the captain murmured. "I'll take your word for it. Do we have time for tea or must we go now?"

There was time.

Minutes went slowly when you were waiting.

Gwyneth was waiting. Excitement lodged in the pit of her stomach, a growing impatience. It wasn't over. It wasn't hopeless. It was gold and bright and had yet to happen. It was not the ending of an old man on the dark mountain. It was the beginning of something. But Enid didn't feel it.

There was a deadness in Enid's face, a deadness Captain Willoughby-Smythe had seen before, on the face of a woman in the slums of Belfast, her whole family shot by terrorists. He had had to tell that woman what she already knew, give substance in words to a grief already formed. When there is love between people, something tells them of life and death. Something told Gwyneth that Rhys and Erlich were alive. Something told Enid the old man was dead. Captain Willoughby-Smythe could not say differently. He laced a mug of tea with brandy and turned to her, squeezed her arm. No matter what happened, her life went on.

"Enid?"

"I am not asleep."

"Drink this."

"I don't need pity."

"It's not pity," the captain said. "It's tea."

"And it's not hopeless either," Gwyneth said roughly.

"No," Enid muttered. "I heard. He is an old man and she gives no chances."

"Who?" said Gwyneth.

"Mawrrhyn."

"Oh," said Gwyneth. "You don't want to believe that rubbish!"

Enid sipped her tea. Her blank stare did not alter.

"You want to think of Rhys," said Gwyneth. "He's alive."

"We'll have a search party out for him at first light," said Captain Willoughby-Smythe.

"Better dead," said Enid. "Like the old man . . . dead and not knowing. And we must wait, always and forever . . . and they have no mercy, star lords and mountains."

"What do you mean?" Gwyneth demanded.

Enid looked at her. "We are alone now, you and me."

"No!"

"He will not be back . . . your brother."

"You can't say that!" Gwyneth shrilled. "Because you don't know! You won't ever know!"

"Ever is more than my lifetime," Enid murmured.

"It's stupid!" said Gwyneth. "Stupid being like that! They're alive, Rhys and Erlich. He's out there somewhere. I'll show you! You just come and see!"

They stood where the gateway gave onto mountains, where there were no steps to show who had gone before them. The snow was smooth and untrodden, a threshold onto emptiness. And empty the Mawrrhyn rose, white and untouched, her great flanks sweeping the sky. They stood together, Enid, Gwyneth, and the man. They did not know what to look for in the vast, barren reaches of the earth and sky. Stars burned their eyes. The pale moon glittered. The wind sang cold as ice and all they could feel was awe.

And it happened like Gwyneth had said it would. There was a faint, distinct humming noise in the sky, south and west toward Cwmvanwy. A humming that grew nearer and louder until it gathered into one great dome of sound. And among the stars something was coming fast. It was white and high and saucer shaped, plunging down, slowing as the color changed from blue to green to a fiery crimson. Low and huge it hung above the moors beyond the Brechin, then it dropped below the ridge and was hidden from their sight.

"A UFO," said Captain Willoughby-Smythe.

"It's come to take Erlich home," Gwyneth told him.

"Never thought I'd ever see one," the man murmured.

It did not stay long. Almost immediately the spacecraft rose, and the humming noise was everywhere, in them and around them, filling all the air. Crimson, green, blue, the sound and the light dragged upward. Powerful, it was. Gripping them, until it veered in a flash of white speed and was gone. Only the stars remained, cold and silent, beautiful and bright.

Gwyneth clutched Enid's arm. Her eyes shone in the moonlight.

"He's done it, Mom! He's going home!"

"Yes," Enid said bleakly.

"It was worth it! It was worth everything, knowing that!"

Worth it . . . Erlich's freedom . . . paid for with a death and a life.

Enid turned back toward the house.

"Aren't you waiting?" Gwyneth asked. "Aren't you waiting for Rhys to come home?"

The house was empty, built of stone, and they could wait out the gray empty years for Rhys to come, but neither she nor Gwyneth would know him again. He was gone. Out there, somewhere. Gone with the star lord through the black velvet distances of space, or gone with the mountain under bog and stone. When there is love between people, something tells them.

"Tell her!" Gwyneth said to the man.

Captain Willoughby-Smythe put an arm around Enid's shoulder.

"Don't give up," he said gently. "Not now."

She touched his hand. She had her life to live and she was not giving up. She was accepting laws that were not hers. She wondered if they loved him . . . Erlich with his gold hair and his freedom, the Mawrrhyn with her rock-scarred soul and her summer flowers. Perhaps in their way they did . . . love . . . Rhys and Hywel Thomas . . . cared in their own way for sheep and stones and stars . . . and a gilt Saint Christopher on a chain.

But loveless and alone on the dark hills, Blod cried for the grief.

24

Blod never did come home. She stayed where they found her that next morning, guarding the mountain in the melting snow, above the place where the old man's body had lain. Gwyneth could not coax her away, and Enid never had loved her. And not for anyone would Blod move. It was as if she must wait there always for Rhys to return. In the lee of a boulder that rose behind her like a great solid door, she sat with her head on her paws, staring down over the valley. Her faith was not pale like human faith. For love of Rhys she would give the only thing she had left to give . . . her life.

But they could not stay for her, Gwyneth and Enid, stay forever in the bleak stone farmhouse at the foot of the mountains, waiting for Rhys to return. They had their own lives to lead. Two years later Enid married Captain Willoughy-Smythe and went to live in Weston-

Super-Mare, and Gwyneth was a nurse in Cardiff General. The farm was left to grow derelict, but Blod was not forgotten by the people of Llanysted. Each day someone would take her food, Cledwyn Hughes, or young Owen-Morgan, or Wynn Evans' children. And Dafydd Jones, who took over the grazing rights after Hywel Thomas, could often be seen of an evening sitting beside her, talking, sharing his supper, or sharing her loneliness. And of course, in the summer the tourists came.

It was ten years since Rhys had disappeared. Ten years Blod waited with her quiet brown patience. The black of her muzzle turned gray. The damp gave her rheumatism. She was old and blind and suffering but she would not relinquish her faith. They talked of having the vet to her out of kindness, but they did not have to. One mild spring morning Dafydd Jones found her dead. For Blod, the waiting was over. He buried her where she had always lived, on the slopes of the Mawrrhyn, and the people of Llanysted paid for a stone to be placed above her grave. It was carved with her name . . . Blod the Dog. And death destroyed even human memory, but the stone waited.

In a cave, Rhys slept and dreamed, woke and slept and dreamed again through a night that seemed endless. He dreamed of a world that was green and warm, feasting and dancing and a woman's face. In dreams he could love her, and the dreams became real because when he woke it was always dark and he was always alone. So he slept because in sleeping he was awake and she was with him with her talk, and her songs, and her wild, wild laughter. He knew who she was: the lady of Mawrrhyn. He knew who he was. But beyond that he could not remember. It was all long ago when he had lived in another dream in another world, and he made no effort to return.

Then he did remember. Suddenly, in a second of pitch-black wakefulness, he remembered Blód was waiting. And it all came tumbling back to him. His mind gripped at the lost reality and held it. There *was* no world in this place below the mountain. Erlich was gone, and he had to go. He had to go . . . home . . . back to Blod, back to his mother. There was nothing stopping him, nothing but a face in a dream that quickly faded.

The underground blackness was not absolute. Ahead of him along a passage through the rock were the gray shades of daylight. Rhys crawled and the light brightened. And then there was sunlight filtering through an opening, a flutter of birds' wings, grass under his hands and tussocks of heather as he heaved himself through. He stood on the slope of the Mawrrhyn. The name of her sang like the tune of a song he could not remember, that fled in the tug of wind through his hair and the fists of the sky beating blue against his eyes.

It was bright, it was morning, and the snow hadn't lasted. The valley was green and brilliant and the view rolled away over fields and villages, out of Wales, into England, green and gold sweeping the world. He had forgotten how beautiful everything was. It was like seeing again after being blind. Overnight it had changed, or he had. Something had been added, an oldness or a newness, a difference he failed to define, in the air, in the world, in himself. He wanted to do nothing more than stand and breathe like a butterfly freshly emerged from the grub of itself, in a pause before flying.

And was it only yesterday since he'd been gone? He didn't know. He felt almost as though a century had passed while he'd been sleeping. Things were changed and not changed. The change wasn't visible. The farmhouse still nestled at the head of the valley. The sheep still grazed on the flanks of the mountains. The same stream tumbled. But never before had Rhys seen or felt it so intensely. Never before had he experienced such perfect freedom. All he needed was someone to share it with . . . a voice, a person, to make it complete.

"Mom!" shouted Rhys. "Blod! Gwyneth! Grandad! I'm back!"

Down below, they wouldn't hear him. Sound rises. But the joy was all welling up inside him and he couldn't wait. He wanted to run headlong down the mountain, take giant leaps over the stones and scree. Run wild, run free, run without thinking. Run! Rhys stopped. There was a gravestone on the bare mountain where none had been before. A gravestone, old and weathered, scabbed with lichen, bearing her name . . . Blod the Dog. And the joy died.

"Blod?" said Rhys. "That's not you, is it?"

He knelt, not believing, traced the letters with his fingers, fought the fear. Blod was dead, buried, his Blod. And only yesterday, only last night, she'd been here, outside, loving him. Blod.

"What have they done?" Rhys asked. "What have they done to me!"

There was nothing to answer him, no one. There was only himself on the Mawrrhyn, and the fear. Blod had died years ago. There was grass on her grave and lichen on the stone. He backed away. He was sick. He was sick inside his head. Sick from the terror.

"Mom!" Rhys screamed as he ran.

They had grown old as he stayed young. A single night and they had lived and died, Enid, Gwyneth, and Hywel Thomas, all of them grown old and died. There was no one left. Nothing. Weeds grew between the cobbles of the yard. The door was gone from the outhouse. The windows gaped. There were holes in the roof where the slates had been, and the paddock was a jungle of burdock and bracken. No one lived here anymore. No one moved or spoke to him. What greeted him at High Valley Farm was silence.

"Mom!" he screamed.

He had never lived through minutes so terrible. Never known what dereliction meant. It seemed to eat right through to his soul. He trod on an empty threshold, across a door fallen from its hinges and splintered with rot. He stood in what had once been the hallway. Fungus grew on the baseboard, nettles thrust through the cracks between the flagstone, cobwebs and dust clung to the remains of the banister, and the floor was dark with droppings. No one lived here, only sheep, only a mouse that scuttled from the smashed body of the clock. And the yellow clock face stared up at him, withered with age and blue speckled with mold. Its black hands were motionless. It would never again strike time. But time struck Rhys like a sword.

If he had ever lived here, it was not in this time. His time was dead, dead like Blod's grave, dead like Gwyneth and Enid and the old man. They were ghosts in his mind who screamed to him out of time. He heard his mother say, There is this place. It will be here when you come back. And it *was* here, a crumbling ruin, a gaunt, creaking skeleton, a terror of utter loneliness.

"No!" Rhys cried. "It can't be! Not like this! Not to me!"

But the Mawrrhyn had no pity.

He sat on the window seat, his head buried in his arms. The day dragged past him filled with sunlight, and the shadow of the Mawrrhyn crept cold down the valley. Perhaps he heard sounds from the outside world, sheep crying on the hills, a farmer whistling to his dogs, a van that bumped up the lane to the forestry cottages, or a plane in the sunset, the hum of its engines making plaster fall from the walls in small flakes. But if he did hear, he gave no sign. He sat still, not seeing, not caring. What happened outside was not in his world or his time.

He was locked alone in a blackness of grief and despair, sealed with the ghosts of a life that he had never even lived. Daylight or darkness, it made no difference to him. Both were empty, both were drained of desire, both were without hope. Dying or crying, he didn't care what he did. There was no one left to make him care.

No one left.

Just footfalls in an empty house.

Rhys raised his head. There were stars beyond the window, and in the lower rooms someone was walking. He listened. A sound, a tread, a flicker of light. Someone was there, someone in the darkness where he thought he was alone. No ghost this, not Enid in the scullery, not the patter of Blod's paws on the stone, but shoes shifting quietly in the stink of sheep. Someone was systematically searching. An old door creaked. A silver radiance flooded the stairway. Then into the crumbling filth of Gwyneth's room Erlich came. Rhys caught his breath.

It was as if time turned backward. Erlich wasn't changed. The blue of his eyes and the gold of his hair were the same as Rhys remembered. He was a star lord. Ageless and beautiful, he could stand and smile. A star lord in all his glory. Silver his clothes, rich and luminous, and the light of his living being shone among the wreck of the room, touched the sadness of broken walls, the piles of plaster and the fallen roof beams. Touching and untouched, Erlich smiled, knowing no grief, no death, and no pity, because he, like the Mawrrhyn, had conquered time.

"You!" said Rhys.

"Yes."

"You? Here? After all this time?"

"What is time? A hundred years more or less."

"A lifetime!"

"They grew old and died," said Erlich. "Can I help it?"

"You came back. Why?"

"I told you I would not forget."

"Why? Why did you come?"

"Would you rather I go?"

"Go . . . to the hell you find me in!"

"I can't do that."

"No more than the Mountain can," Rhys said bitterly.

"Must I pretend grief I cannot feel? The laws of nature are not of my making. They lived and were happy. Your mother had another child. . . ."

"I don't want to know!" Rhys howled. "Go, if that's why you've come here! I don't want filling in! I don't want to know all the past history I've missed. I wanted to live it! But I paid! I paid for you . . . with a life sentence! And now I go on living and they're dead! And you, in your freedom, stand there and tell me . . ."

Erlich turned, leaned against the lintel of the door. His eyes lifted skyward. Stars shone on his face, and Rhys fell silent. There was no point in talking. Words could not reach through that kind of distance, could not touch a star lord with no soul.

"We are cruel," Erlich murmured. "We are made that way, she and I. Natural forces pay no heed to the pains of people. She is mountain born, her soul rooted in rock, and I belong to the stars. But my power is not like her power, uncontrolled and indiscriminate, destroying all in its path, by earthquake, fire, and avalanche. Science gives me the ability to choose. So I choose not to destroy. I choose to come back for you."

"What?" said Rhys.

Erlich swung around, eyes, burning blue, bored into Rhys.

"I choose to come back for you," Erlich said. "Because I am not a mountain, not devoid of compassion. You may owe your life to that mountain, but I owe my life to you and I choose not to leave you here alone. And there is no hell, except in a mind that struggles against a power greater than itself. So look . . . up there . . . and tell me what you see."

"Stars," Rhys said levelly without looking up.

"Heaven," said Erlich. "A heaven of worlds . . . my world . . . your world . . . beautiful and existing, waiting for both of us . . . If you'll come."

Rhys stared. Around Erlich's neck hung the gilt Saint Christopher, a tarnished pendant on a tarnished chain.

Some powers were greater than star lords or mountains. Maybe they'd know that . . . Enid and Gwyneth, the old man and Blod. And the Mawrrhyn rose stark and lonely over the land of Wales. But perhaps even she loved in her way the flowers of the bog myrtle, the bones of the sheep, the soul of a boy and a dog.